Borough Wars

By Jonathan Capichano

Edited by Nicole Hoy and Jason Wisniewski

Artwork by Derek Morison

Introduction

When writing this I didn't just want to make a sequel to the last book. I wanted to support local artists and comedians. Without these people in my life, my world would be dull and boring. Many of these comics are extremely talented, so I asked them for their input and for some good roast jokes. I hope to help out my community and show the rest of NY some of what we have to offer.

Special thanks.

First, I want to thank all my friends for giving me inspiration to write. Thank you to the Comedians around NYC who supplied some of the Jokes within this book. You'll see their names within the book itself and links to some of their material in the back.

A big thank you to the veterans who gave me insight on how a chain of command would work in a world where the government has collapsed.

I would like to thank Brooke Levy. You helped me when most people wouldn't. My life was falling apart till you came. You pushed me to keep going when others said to quit. You pulled me back up when I fell on hard times. You made me laugh when life threw its worst at me. If you didn't come into my life when you did, I wouldn't have been able to move forward with my dreams of becoming a writer. I'm sorry things didn't work out and ended the way they did. I do hope to talk to you again someday.

Thank you, Nikki Lee, for all the edits and criticism. You made sure that my work came to life in ways I wouldn't have thought of.

Jason Wisniewski you helped me from the start. Any time I needed advice you always put down whatever it is you were doing looked over and criticized my work. Then pushed me to do more. You're a good friend and a tough teacher.

Derek Morison. Thank you for doing the artwork for this book. You're an inspiration to artists everywhere.

Prologue

The stars were barely visible through the trees. Not that the two Brooklyn Knights needed the light. The fires from the shoreline brightened the night sky well enough so they could make out where they were going. Both were dragging a Navy sea bag. A trail was left behind them of mud and pebbles. Grime, debris and some animal feces was dragged along with the bag itself.

"Come on Duke. I think this a good enough spot as any."

"Yeah ok. Dump him."

Grabbing the bottom of the bag and dumping the man headfirst onto the dirt, groaning as he hit the floor. Duke and the other Brooklyn Knights laughed at his pain.

"Well look at that. He got his duct tape off his mouth. Take a good look at the light asshole. Your town is burning. We want information, and your goanna give it to us. So anything you wanna tell me before I start feeding you your teeth?"

Caps looks at the fires in the distance. Trying to adjust his eyes to the light he blinks a few times. He then stares at the blazing houses. He listens to the gun fire, the car tires screeching as the rubber and pavement grind against each other in the distance. The screams of people in pain. Even from this distance he could make out some words.

One of the Brooklyn Knight's loses his patience. Using a knife, he took from a dead Staten Islander, he starts pointing it at the fires in the distance. Then grabs Caps by the shirt collar and yells into his ear.

"Look here cum dumpster! You and your crew of faggaty ass Staten Island tree huggers lost. We own this town, we own you! Now tell us where you keep your stash of supplies!" He then takes a knee and is now in his face. His foul-smelling breath is amplified by the warmth felt on the captive's face. "Maybe you live. Now . . . start . . . talking!"

Then the Brooklyn Knight quickly cut Caps cheek. Caps jerks his head in the opposite direction to avoid the blade as best he could. The knife wielding Brooklyn Knight laughed. Then the other one says "You got nothing to say huh?

Caps looks around him and listens. He look's left, then right, then smiles widely. He knows where he is. And what they just walked into.

"The fuck you smiling at cock sucker!" Duke shouts.

Suddenly lights turn on all around them. The Brooklyn Knight look around in every direction and pull out their pistols. They shout, “Mother fuckers! Put down your weapons mother fuckers!”

The Brooklyn knights see a dozen shadowy figures. All with bows and rifles pointed at them. The shadowy figures don’t say anything.

“You shit heads want us? Huh?!” The two Brooklyn Knight’s shouted as some of the shadowy figure walked towards them.

Too busy pointing their guns at everything that walked towards them, they don’t realize that Caps untied himself. He then stands up behind them and puts on his glasses. They both turn around in a frantic panic and point their guns at him. Each of their reflections shines in a lens of his glasses. They see the fear they are showing.

Caps keeps smiling and says calmly. “I got something to say. You boys make a lot of noise. You forget where you are? Welcome to the quiet borough.”

Chapter 1

Mac was standing up straight with his chest out. He was showing that Army bravado that he always showed right before he gave out a plan. Pretty hard to do when his beer gut was showing every time, he stood up straight; he stood on the gym bleachers with two American flags on each side of him.

“Everyone! Gather around!”

A crowd of ragtag people came in close and formed a circle around him and sat Indian style on the floor. Everyone had some sort of weapon on them. Rifles, pistols, butcher’s knife’s, kitchen knives. Some even had homemade weapons.

“Alright ladies and gentlemen. We’re going on another scavenger hunt. Last group cleared out Tottenville, Rossville, and Bloomingdale. Next, we are going to the shores near New Dorp. Same drill as always. Look for survivors, but most importantly look for supplies”

Pauline raises her hand to ask a question. Mac points in recognition.

“So, we finally going back to the hospital?”

“Yes, Pauline we’re going back. This time in force. But you’re not going”

Pauline turns red and stands up in a fury. She steps over two people in front of her and yells at Mac.

“OK, WHAT THE FUCK! Last two missions’ you guys had me stay on base and just watch the fucking water for boats! I wanna get out of here and see what else I can do! I’m useful God Dammit!”

Mac points to her outfit and says, “Not when you’re dressed like a confused teenager who looks like she used to it was ok to try on all the edible underwear in hot topic.”

The crowd around them laughs. Pauline, though angry, can’t help but laugh at the comment. The room suddenly goes quiet when Butch walks in, pulling a chalkboard with maps taped to it. The door he came through shutting loudly when he let go. The door isn’t what made everyone stare. He’s a giant of a man. Over six feet tall, he towers over most people in the room.

“Ok guys. I’m just waiting for Hope” He then leans over to Mac and says “Sorry sir, Hope is in the bathroom. Her chlamydia is acting up again. I’ll run over and tell that I Hope she gets better soon but to hurry the fuck up.”

Mac paused and stared at Butch for a moment that seemed longer than it actually was. Then leaned forward and whispered in his ear.

"Was that a name pun?"

"Uh. . . Yes sir"

"That was so bad it was good kind of good. So just find her and I'll let it go."

Butch smiles and walks off back through the door where he came from. Again, it slams shut and makes some of the people sitting jump.

Mac then gets loud. His voice amplified by the emptiness of the room. His plan seemed more like gaining intel rather than a well laid out plan.

"Ok!" Mac's voice boomed through the room. "We're going to run through each of the four buildings off of Seaview Avenue and see what we can get," he points to the map on the chalkboard. "First building will be hit by my team: J Squad. Second building will be hit by Darin's S Squad. Third building will be hit by-"

"By D squad, right?" Pauline interrupted with a raised hand.

"There's a joke about guy running a train on you somewhere. . . Ok ladies and gentlemen, get your shit together and be ready by nineteen hundred!" Mac orders loudly.

Pauline then asks. "Why can't you just say seven o'clock? We're not military"

Mac shakes his head before responding. "Shut up Pauline" Then looks back up. "Ok everyone gets your shit together. You have one hour."

Everyone stands up and shouts "Err Rah!" before heading for the exit or going back to their duties. All except one. Caps was sitting high upon the crates of food nearby. He jumped down, landing into a crouch before standing back up.

Pauline walks up to him with excitement "You're back! You find it?"

Caps reaches into his back and pulls out a box of tampons and a big bag of Recess, "I figure one should go with the other"

She hugs him and says, "You always do try to make a bad situation into a good one. Eh Johnny boy?" Then noticing the serious look he was trying to hide from Mac she then starts to walk away.

"I'll let you boys talk"

As soon as Pauline walks out the door, Caps locks it behind her. He then takes a deep breath and walks up to Mac.

“There’s something wrong with the plan Mac.” Caps says calmly.

“No there isn’t. All scouts said the same thing. No dead heads, no infected, no trouble. Just a bunch of bodies decaying.”

“That’s my point!” Caps says with a boom in his voice. “Those bodies are fresh. They didn’t start decaying months ago. Only recently. Someone shot them point blank in the head. There were bullet casings everywhere! We’re not the-”

“That’s enough!” Mac screams.

The people that remained in the Gym room began to stare. Mac put his arm around Caps and began to forcefully walk to the door with him. He stops and looks back at the people who were staring at them. The people quickly realizing that he sees them, turn their heads and go back to what they were doing before. Then he turns his attention to Caps and points at him.

“Look, we can’t keep sitting on our hands and knees waiting for help. There’s no one coming. We’re burning through food, water and medical supplies. If anything, finding other people will be helpful. We can trade with them, build with them, and-"

Not wanting to look him in the face but wanting to express his opinion Caps rolls his eyes before looking away in disgust, then replying, "Or they can kill us. Those bodies were wearing tactical gear. Vests made to hold magazines of rifle ammunition. Very few of them were wearing scrubs and doctors' coats. You ask me looks like they were attacked by another group, or worse."

Mac paused and glared at Caps before repeating the last word he heard. "Worse?"

"They were betrayed. The gates where supply trucks loaded shipments of all sorts, those bodies were shot in the back. The rest must have caught on and started shooting back but it looks like only a few of them got a chance to use their weapons. It was a fucking massacre. Then they were shot in the head to make sure they stayed dead. "

Mac looked at him and rested on a nearby crate to think. His hand to his forehead and elbow on top of the crate he leaned on, he fell silent, deep in thought. He knew Caps was right. There was another group out there, the question that kept coming up in Mac's head was "where are they?" He had scouts are all over Staten Island. Thoughts of logistics came into play. How did a group large enough to do grab supply's, kill the mass of dead in that hospital, and have a gun fight, while not get spotted?

Meanwhile Caps stood there with his arms now crossed. He took the hint to calm down and take a breath. He then turned around and leaned against the crate with Mac. Caps stared at the wall and said "I'll find 'em. I'll try to see what we're up against. A group with that much fire power, is definitely not from a quiet neighborhood. I'm betting they like to show off their strength. Let's not worry about whose got more firepower for now"

Mac replies, "I'm worried more about our own mistakes than any plans from whatever potential enemies we have."

Caps looks at him puzzled. "What you mean by our own mistakes?"

"Nothing. Forget I said anything. Look you been scavenging houses and cars for days. When was the last time you slept? I sent you out three days ago."

"I try to get some sleep here and there." He says while fighting the urge to yawn and failing.

He takes out one of his five-hour energy shots from his pocket. Mac grabs it out of his hand before he could open it.

“Go get some rest. You’ve earned it. Besides. I know your girl misses you.”

Caps smiles and takes back his energy shot. Putting it in his pocket he replies, “Alright” He says while yawning again, “I’ll see you in the morning.”

Chapter 2

Paradise

Walking back inside his Room on the far end of the building, Caps throws off his muddy shoes and doesn't wait to take off his clothes. He walks right over, and lands face down into his bed. While making a tiring noise he puts his arm around his girlfriend Paige and with a smirk, holds her tight and says "mine"

She turns around, saying in excitement, "Hi baby"

He puts his hand around her waist and starts pulling her closer. She embraces his kiss. Her bright blue eyes were visible thanks to the moon light shining through the small window.

"Hi old man! I missed you"

Caps being able to only keep his eyes halfway open, doesn't reply. Just smiles and thinks how lucky he is. He reminded himself how he owed her so much before the world ended. And then how soon, he was going to make it all up to her. They both fall back to sleep. He never let's go.

Morning has come and Caps wakes up to the smell of bacon and eggs.

“How did you sneak that past the supply guards? He asked as he nearly trips while getting up.

“As the leader of the supplies department, you’d be surprised at what I can get away with.”

Caps looks at her with a smile replying, “Let me guess, extra rations? You know you shouldn’t give that guy Frank anything right? He’s kind of weird. I don’t trust him”

“You don’t trust anyone. Especially if they’re men.” Paige replies with a smirk.

Caps just smiles. He sits down at the table and fixes the plates. He keeps looking back at her and smiling. Stopping what he’s doing, he walks up to her and holds her from behind and kisses her on the head. “I love you. . . but I still don’t like your mother”

“Oh jeez. What’d she do now?”

Letting go of her and going back to setting up the table he replies, “Just gave me a dirty look last night.”

“What did you do?”

“Nothing”

Paige then turns and looks to him tilting her head slightly with an expression that screams (oh really). Caps smiles and replies with one of his bad jokes.

"Ok well I told her I would convert for you."

"AW! You did!? . . . wait; what did you do to make her mad then?"

Caps puts his hands up, smiles and say's "Well I said I was already halfway there since my bald head looks like its circumcised from the beard up."

Paige laughs loudly and hugs him while asking, "You'd really convert? Aren't you an atheist?"

"Agnostic, but after what you said about your mom being uncomfortable with her Christian grandson being baptized, I think it would be easier for her. This way she's happy with me and that makes you happy".

Paige hugs him tight and looks up at him with her big blue eyes. "You're too much, you know that?"

"I try. Just wish we didn't have to do the whole circumcision thing."

She looks up at him "What?"

"Just the whole cutting off part of the penis. . . It's just odd."

Paige rolls her eyes with a smirk knowing he's about to have a bad argument that's more of a joke. But listens knowing he's just trying to make her smile.

"I'm just saying it's weird that we still do it. I mean, I understood why Jews first started it. They were desert people and sand got everywhere. Circumcision made it easier to not get so itchy."

Paige smiles, puts her head on his chest. She listens to his heartbeat and says "Just shut up and hold me"

He kisses her head with closed eyes. One of hers though weren't. She sees past him and looks at the slightly opened door. A figure stood there and smiled. He had heavy eyelids and a slightly receding hairline. Noticing he's been seen he backs away. Paige says nothing as her smile fads. She turns back to the stove and keeps finishes cooking. As Caps grabs forks and knifes, Paige takes one last look at the door and walks over to it, turns the knob and quietly shuts the door. She then walks back to the kitchen with a small nervous look on her face. Looking back at Johnny she shakes it off and finishes cooking.

"So, what's going on today? You're almost never here." Paige says with food in her mouth.

Caps just looks up, trying to avoid eye contact so he doesn't show his expression over the bad news.

"I'm not going to lie to you. We might have a fight on our hands. Someone raided the hospital on Seaview. We found bodies. Lots of them. All not from this borough."

Paige stops chewing and looks at him without blinking. She can sense the worry in his voice. He was good at hiding his emotions from others. But she could tell when he was angry, sad, and scared. He didn't jitter or stutter when frightened. He was calm. He seemed to act as if he was planning on what to do next. He was known for reacting fast to problems. Only a few times he would blow up in anger if things got to out of hand.

"When?"

Caps looks up from his plate and replies. "When? When what?" He sees her eyes look heavy with tears forming.

"When are you leaving? I don't see you for days. You never even bring me back anything anymore."

Caps gets up and holds her. "I'm sorry. What do you want? I'll go find it."

She pushes him away, she replies with a higher tone, "I heard you brought Pauline stuff. Did you even think of me?"

Caps just stands there looking puzzled. Not knowing what he did wrong, he listens.

"You always go out with them when you have free time. We never have fun anymore."

Paige turns in the other direction to not look at him. Caps can sense how hurt she is. He spends days sometimes almost weeks away looking scouting and scavenging for supplies. He tries to apologize.

"I know I'm sorry. I've just been busy is all. I'm trying to make sure we have a future. Things are getting better and you see that." He digs into his pocket and pulls out a chain. He wraps it around her neck.

She jumps and pushes away saying, "What the fuck are you. . .!" She then looks and sees a Star of David on the chain. It was a white gold necklace with diamond studs on the star. Paige's eyes widen as Caps puts in on her.

"You really think I forgot about you? There's an apocalypse happening out there. This isn't like when we used to go to comedy clubs all the time. It's more like I'm busy like I was with school. Except I kill the infected and not my GPA. Look, I'm going to ask to change occupation so I can be with you more. Ok?"

Paige looks at his eyes. She then wipes her tears, "No more scouting? No more of waiting to see you for days or a week at a time?"

He looks at her and pulls her closer again. "That's right. You know me. If I see a problem, I try to fix it. Now we can hang out with your friends and mine and go out and have fun again. I'll ask Mac to put me on logistics, so I'm closer to you. After I get rid of this headache."

Just then the radio on Caps belt goes off. Two beeps mean's its Mac. He closes his eyes and takes a deep breath in and out. He then looks down at Paige and say's "Give me a second". He then walks over to the door and leans on it with one arm.

"This is Johnny Caps."

"I know this is a bit soon for you brother, but I need you to go out again for one night. Come to my office. We'll discuss it more there."

Caps looks towards Paige. She was packing his breakfast before he even finished speaking on the radio. "I'm sorry. But. . . "

"I know. Dead heads don't die on their own. Go. I'll wait for you here. Take some food with you. You haven't eaten. It will help with your headache."

She hands him a Tupperware with bacon, eggs, silver dollar pancakes and syrup in McDonalds packages. Then turns around and starts doing the dishes. Her face is blood red. She's trying to hold back the tears. Just then she's hugged from behind and kissed on the cheek. "I really don't know what I'd do without you"

Paige smiles and Caps walks out the door. Once the door is shut Paige walks over locks it, and then takes a chair and wedges it shut. Walking over to the kitchen table she sits down and with her hand over her face she starts to cry. Sadness and anger start to fill her head.

After a few minutes of intense emotions, she looks to her plant in the corner. She gets up and walks over to it. Opening the garden gnome at the foot of the plant she pulls out a small radio. She checks the time and then turns it on to a signal that only she and one other knows.

"I'm alone. Come over"

Chapter 3

Two days earlier

A tanned skinned bald man with a Ginny tee walks into the room, gently leaning a golf club on his shoulder. He has scars going down his arm and half a pinky finger missing. He stops and looks at everyone in the school's gym before shouting, "Listen up faggots! I am Louis. AKA, Your BAD ASS captain! We gather here today to survive and plan. We" While smiling with a big grin on his face, he pauses and points his club at the right side of the room, "have fresh blood from Manhattan with us today! Now I know we had out differences in the past, but that's water under the Brooklyn bridge, or the Manhattan bridge. Sensing the awkwardness, he made with his last comment he clears his throat with a fake cough and gets to the point. "Or whatever bridge you want. They will be our loaders."

Louis, AKA, BAD ASS captain points his golf club at a poorly drawn map on the brick wall behind him. "We are going to what should be New Jersey. The forgotten borough of Staten Island" He then goes to the center of the room and opens his arms. "Brooklyn Knights! We are going to take whatever THE FUCK WE WANT! CAN YOU DIG IT?!"

Everyone in the room at the same time gives a loud “ER RAH!”.

He then paces back and forth in front of both groups, making slight swinging gestures to see who flinches. None of the Brooklyn Knights flinch. The Manhattanizes did. Some even took a step back. A look of disappointment was vividly expressed across the face of Captain badass. “Who would have thought that the group that gave us trouble would be so God dam twitchy.”

“Didn’t help that you killed some of our best men!” A female voice yells out from the Manhattan crowd.

“Who the fuck said that!” Captain Louis moving through the ranks grabbing individuals and demanding to know if it was them. None answered.

“Fucking pussy! You shout shit like that again and I’ll-“

“At ease Louie. I know who it was” A Elderly man with dark brown skin and silver fox hair and matching goatee interrupts while walking into the room. He orders everyone to sit down. Louis and the Brooklyn Knights take a Knee”

“You should have been paying more attention to the troops we have here instead of trying to scare them. Now I have to remind you why you were demoted."

He takes out his knife and Louis starts to beg. "No please sir, not another one"

Everyone one on the Manhattan side watched in aww as Louis went from the toughest man to one that was now groveling, crying, he started kissing the man's right foot. He then puts his knife away, mocking him as he does so.

"That's better. Now let me show what happens when you don't pay attention"

Louis looks up only for blood to be splattered on him. The old man shot the women to his right.

"You never bothered to think it was a man who shouted at you now did you?"

Louis looked at the old man confused. The women he shot was dressed in men's clothes and even had some facial hair. "Sir I-"

"She was Trans. You would have seen that if you inspected the gang beforehand instead of trying to copy the speech from the warrior's movie. Looks like she had run out of treatments." He says as he wipes the blood off Louise's cheek.

The elderly man walks away leaving Louie standing there with everyone staring at him. He slowly walks towards the front of the room and stares out the window. Sensing the awkwardness, he coughs to clear the lump in his throat, then turns around and screams, "OH KAY BABY SHIT STANES! Get your shit together!" We're moving out!"

A Few Hours Later

"Come on limp shits! Move your asses!" Louie shouts while acting like his alter ego Captain Badass. He drives around the three hospital buildings, bossing around the Manhattan crew as they load all three straight trucks with medical equipment and supplies. The Brooklyn Knights have a small skeleton crew helping but mostly stand guard for any infected that might come their way.

First was the mental health section. Louie and three other cars parked in front of the main entrance. On Louie's signal they each start to honk their horns. Three and four at a time start to stumble out through the front doors. The infected are attracted to the noise, like moths to a flame. Twenty Brooklyn Knights stand in a line and eight Manhattan Knights form one in front of them taking a knee. As the dead come for the noise, the Knights open fire.

A chatter of all types of machine guns, rifles, and handguns can be heard from the other buildings.

This was just one building out of many. Each section of Seaview hospital had its own set of buildings for a specific reason. One is the mental hospital, another for dialysis, and the last for surgeries. The Mental hospital area had one main building in the center with two floors. The front end of the building was a wall of windows on the first floor and second. With a red roof in between the floors and a Red slanted roof on the top. The leader of the Manhattan knights ordered his men to stop opening the door for the dead to walk out of. He ordered the cars to turn on their bright and shine the lights into the building and honk their horns.

Bodies started to group together against the windows. Each of them trying to claw and bite their way through. Then the Manhattan knight gave the order to open fire on the second floor.

Louie steps next to the Manhattan knight. “You know Plexiglass windows don’t shatter, right?”

Manhattan knight doesn’t turn but stares at the windows “but they do break apart with force. Look.”

The infected started to break through each window. The Plexiglass bended and broke with each body that pushed up against it. Soon the dead were slowly falling out of the top windows and sliding on the roof and to the ground. Some breaking a bone while others just got back up with no effect on them.

Louie then pulled out his bullhorn "Fucking shoot God dammit!"

Everyone opened fire at the same moment. None were aiming for the head. Most waisted their ammunition by just firing left to right. Louie then steps out of his car. Walks up to one of the Manhattan knights and takes his handgun. Turns and fires a round point blank into an infected head. "Shoot for the head you bunch of dumbasses." He said with frustration in his voice. Many of the dead were now getting back up. The two lines reloaded and started firing in single shots and short bursts.

Over 20 minutes of constant shooting the dead were not coming out. Nothing was left inside. Louie gave the signal and both Brooklyn and Manhattan knights grabbed the carts they brought with them. Louie sits in his car, checking the time.

He picks up his radio and says "You got twenty minutes to grab everything you can and get out.

Right on time everyone filled up their carts and ran back out and loaded the trucks.

Next was the Northwell hospital. Louie sent men to surround all entrances and exits. The main force was once again to move through the main entrance. This building was shaped like a "V". The building was irregular. Each wing had a different number of floors and almost all the windows had its shades down. Making it harder to know how many infected there might be in the building.

Again, Louie ordered two lines with the Manhattan knights in front. Once again, they turned on the cars headlights and blasted their horns. Window shades started to shake, and the pounding of windows could be heard from the top floor. But none were breaking.

The captain of the Manhattan knights was a Skinny man with a mole between his eyebrows. He ran up to Louie and said loudly "If most are locked in their rooms then we can clear it out one by one."

Louie signaled with his hand for everyone to stop honking their horns and turn off their lights. He stepped out of the car and looked at the captain. "That's a dumb fucking idea!" He said with a boom in his voice. "We are here for the medicine. We are not a fucking clean up crew. Is that understood? Now get your men in there and raid the shit out of it."

With that order the Manhattan Knights once again grabbed their carts and moved in. The Brooklyn Knights waited outside and stood watch for anything that came out the main entrance dead.

Chapter 4

Contact

Sitting by the shoreline with two 18 wheelers trucks to their right, and left, and a fire truck stuck in the water in front of them. The semi box these made, made the Manhattan skyline look like they were seeing it from a movie theater. Pauline, and Sabrina sat on the hood of the Jeep, with Caps sitting in the driver's seat.

Sabrina was holding binoculars and watching for signs of life. She checks the windows of any building she can get a good look at. Murphy sits next to her with a pen and paper. Sabrina calls out the room and the floor and describes what she sees.

"Dead head on the 10th floor 4th window to the right. Bluish building, no wait, three dead heads"

Caps pulls out the file he's been keeping in his backpack. He puts it on top of Pauline's clipboard. Both The two ladies stop what they're doing and read it. It says "Be advised, starting today we are looking out for live potential threats. Look for any signs of automatic. Watch for flashlights and cars that are not of our own. Pauline was about to say something when Caps cuts her off,

“I know, it’s a pointless order”

“Ya think!?” Sabrina shouted. “Like we’re already pretty much doing that. Is that why you’re here? To make sure we’re doing our job?”

Caps looks at her and with a head tilt he says, “Kind of.”

“What you mean kind of?”

“Sal says your reports have been lacking substance. You ladies were the closest to the Verrazano bridge. You didn’t see any cars cross over it?”

“Not a single one. We would have heard it too.”

Caps looked at them with disappointment. He reaches into the glove compartment and pulls out two pairs of headphones. “This is why you didn’t hear them crossing. You guys are watching the city while listening to music.”

Both just look at Caps. Sabrina with some anger, Murphy with some regret. Sabrina snatches the headphones out of Caps’ hands and throws them in the water.

“Happy?”

Pauline gasps and says “Those were his. I borrowed them a month ago”. Sabrina’s eyes widened. “Sorry” Caps doesn’t reply. Just looks at his headphones sinking in the water. A moment passes and he turns around and says “Let’s take a break. Listen to some music. . . on low, ok?”

A sigh of relief left Sabrina’s lungs. Caps was known for his little temper when things broke or were wasted. Pauline pulls out the cooler from the trunk and sets it aside. Then pulls out an iPod music player. Her play list starts off with Bob Marley’s music. She then reaches into the bottom of the cooler and pulls out a bag of weed. Sabrina shouts “You know me so well!” Pauline smiles and offers Caps some, but he says “Last time I smoked I had to drive. I kept waiting at stops signs for them to turn green so I can go. I’ll just do your job for few”

Pauline just smirks shakes her head and starts rolling a blunt. She tries to make some small talk.

“So how’s things going with you and Paige? You pop the question yet?”

Caps face turns a little red. Pauline knew that too get on Caps good side they just needed to talk about Paige. It was a conversation they had before. He had his grandmothers ring already cleaned up and polished by his cousin Pete.

"You always smile more when we talk about her. You guys are cute together."

"The air smells differently since the world ended, doesn't it?" Sabrina asks out loud as she unties her hair and lets it wave about.

Pauline does the same "Yeah I noticed that too. Hey, Caps you smell that?"

"Sorry, couldn't hold it"

Sabrina turns around in disgust. "We were talking about the air. Not the fart you were cooking up. You're fucking nasty you know that?"

Caps with a smirk "My bad. Not like you can smell it from here. No wind cause of these trucks." Caps points to the fire truck.

"Hey Pauline, you took the fire firefighter exam, right? What score did you get?"

"Don't know, don't care"

"You're not even curious?"

Pauline's cheeks turn red and she smiles. "Not really. Lots of cute guys taking the exam though. So, I didn't really care if I got into the fire department, so long as some of the department got into me"

Both Caps and Sabrina roll their eyes.

All three go back out to staring in the distance. The air was warm. Small bursts of cool ocean air moved in between the two trucks, and the noise of the wind was amplified from bouncing off the trucks. Caps turns his hat forward to block the sun. It's an old brown coppola.

Caps starts looking through the binoculars and notices something odd. "Hey where's all the dead heads?"

"Their around. Just not many left I guess"

Sabrina lifts off his hat and holds it above him and say's "You're such an old man you know that!" As Caps tried to get his hat back, Pauline walks behind the truck to defecate. She stays within ear shot of them. She can hear them arguing like children. As she's peeing, she looks at the shadows on the floor. The trees close by were in a row and sway back in forth in the wind. Made it look almost like a dance. One shadow didn't move. Then suddenly it started to move toward her. She screams to the top of her lungs and tries to run, but trip's over her own shorts. Sabrina and Caps run towards her direction and see her being gagged and pulled into a Jeep. Both of them pull out their pistols. Sabrina yells out

“AIM FOR THE TIRES!”. As they fire, they manage to shoot out the back-left tire. The kidnappers fire back. One with an Ak47, the other with a pump action shotgun. Caps leaps behind one of the tires of the truck. Sabrina tries to find cover but is shot in the left side of her hip and between her shoulder blades. Caps tries to keep the kidnappers busy with more gun fire so Sabrina can crawl away to safety. But it’s no use. She falls to her knees, looks up and takes one hard last breath. Then dies sitting up with her arms to her side and palms facing up.

The doors shut and the Jeep drives away. Caps rolls out and shoots at the right-side tire. But runs out of ammo. He tries to reload but can’t get the clip out of his belt. “Damn it!” He shouts. His mind begins to race as the Jeep is lost in sight. Caps can’t control his emotions. Sadness and anger were twisting in his stomach.

Caps hears shuffling near him. He turns to see Sabrina now standing up. “Oh shit” She turns around and starts sprinting towards him.

He runs to the car and turns it on. Sabrina jumps in and tries to grab him but stumbles into the seats headfirst. Caps gets the convertible to raise its roof and entraps Sabrina in the car. He jumps back out of the front seat quickly. He falls on his ass and slams the door with his foot. He then stood up facing the car, watching as Sabrina pounds the window with the palms of her hands, as if she's trying to grab him through the glass. His attention then goes back to the road the kidnappers went down.

Pulling out his radio he turns to HQ frequency. "This is Caps. We have a situation. Asking for a pickup at shoreline bird watch. Over! . . . Bring a tow truck."

Chapter 5

A girl's worst nightmare

Kicking and screaming through her gag Pauline does everything she can to cause as much damage as possible. Three of them were trying to hold her down. First, they held her arms behind her back and wrapped duct tape around her writs. She manages to get her gag off and bites one of them on his upper thigh.

"You fucking bitch! Ah! Get this cunt off me!" the man yells.

She bites so close to his penis that he screams just as much from the panic than the actual bite. He pulls her off by the hair and ears. The man sitting next in the front seat reaches back and ties duct tape around her mouth and face as quickly as he can. First wrap around went over her nose and eye, do to the fighting. Second wrapped around her mouth. Third time was on point. The duct tape was then passed to the man behind the passenger seat. He grabbed her ankles and pulled her legs to his chest. The other two men then took the tape and wrapped it around her ankles.

Suddenly sparks could now be seen outside the window. The tire that was shot out was now on its rim. Pulling over, the driver who is a short man with brown skin and has hair as black as the tires, jumps out and shouts “Get her out while I change the tire. I need five minutes! Control this bitch!” Just then they get out and pull Pauline out by her legs. She hits her head on the bottom of the car door and street. She only has one nostril to breathe out of and its now bleeding

The driver runs to the back and takes out the spare. Pauline tries to scratch the duct tape off her wrists. But her fingernails can’t reach. One of the captive’s notices. He’s a large man with a receding hair line, with the rest of his remaining hair slicked back. His teeth are a yellowish color from smoking. He quickly walks over, combs his hair back, then grabs her hand, pulls out a hammer, and breaks the finger she was using. As she screams in pain.

“Shh, shh, shh. We’re going to take good care of you little one” He says as he grabs her ass.

Pauline then frails around trying to get his hand off of her. The pervert just keeps grabbing as she tries to get away. Giggling as he does.

“Tires fixed. Let’s get moving! Back in the car now!” The pervert doesn’t care. He just keeps feeling up Pauline. Tears started running down her face as the feeling of helplessness takes over.

"What the fuck are you doing? Mike get Michael off of her so we can get going"

Others started to then question why Mike the creep was even brought along. "Seriously who the fuck told this asshole to join us?"

Mike pulls Michael off of her and pushes him back. "Get in the passenger side. Now!" The original person in the passenger seat, a man named Mitch helps bring Pauline in the car. She now sits in the middle of the two in the back seat. Shaking with adrenaline pushing through her system. As the driver starts the engine Michael looks over and blows Pauline a kiss. The driver stares at him with disgust. Michael just keeps staring at Pauline till the driver slaps him. "Eyes forward jerkoff". Michael is annoyed but undeterred. He then tries to look at Pauline with the rearview mirror. "What the fuck did I just say!?" Finally realizing the tension, he was causing, Michael looks away.

Starting the car and speeding as fast as he can Mike loudly says to Michael, "I'm reporting you to the head honcho. You deserve desk job for this shit. You're sick in the fucking head."

Michael just smiles widely with his crooked yellow teeth. He knows something they don't. But doesn't say anything. Known by the top dogs for keeping secretes, Michael is one of the secret guards the Brooklyn Knights are known for having. His job is to see who the toughest and most ruthless of the gang squads are. He knows any report they submit won't see the light of day. Because he's in charge of who gets to see those reports.

Chapter 6

Arthur Kill Correctional Facility

Intel, plan, revenge

Second in command James Mac and five other officers sit at the oval table. No one says anything to each other. All are internally questioning the meeting. Though they all know why they're here. It's with what happened at the hospital.

One of the officers named Collin tried to break the ice with some small talk.

"Hard to believe how lucky we got. No prisoners were left when this was taken over huh?" But they left the goats?

Mac answers "No. This place closed before the apocalypse. It was being made into a movie production studio. Broadway studios, I think. Goats are there to keep the grass cut and to eat all the poison ivy".

"That explains this room" Collin replies while slowly spinning in his chair admiring the room and its fancy filming equipment. Collin puts both hands, palm side down on the desk to stop his spinning before asking the room, "So does anyone else notice that the survival guide we got is almost the same as every other survival guide?

Mac rolling his eyes answers quickly. “That’s because preparing for any apocalyptic event has the same preparedness. Stockpile resources, protection community and communication. Now let’s just sit here quietly before the commander walks in.”

Almost as if on Qu Commander Sal Caladonato walks in. Everyone stands up. “At ease, please sit” With that command everyone sits, except for Caladonato. He turns on his computer with a projector pointing at the wall. Images of the bodies from the hospital are shown.

“Thoughts anyone?” James Mac is the first to speak up. “One of our scouts say it was an execution. Though not there to see it, I believe him.”

A rebuttal is then aimed at Mac from one of the other officers. “What makes you think this one scout is right? Could just be another one who thinks he will get extra rations for being smart.”

Stands up and pointing at the projection on the wall, Mac says “Look at how the bodies are laying down. They are facing the hospital. Not facing away. Someone used them, then executed them.”

Commander Caladonato looks towards the officers and then towards the projection. “Your right. Most of them are shot in the back. No one has picked up any radio chatter?”

Everyone in the room was silent. Some looked at the board. Others looked down at the desk in front of them. Everyone felt that they haven’t been doing their jobs.

“I’m assigning a team to look just for radio chatter. Mac I need you to assign one of your scouts to go to Todd hill and get control over the radio tower.”

Mac smiles and says “I know just the man for the job. I’ll get Jacob right on it. His team should. . . “Sal cuts him off “You didn’t get the report yesterday?” Mac looks at his commander Puzzled.

“Moreen!”

Moreen shuffles through the door and peeks her head into the room “Yes commander?”

“Can you please do your job and hand our second in command the file about Jacob?

She quickly runs to her desk. Shuffling of paperwork could be heard through the opening of the slowly closing door. She then runs in and hands Mac the file. It’s a short list of scouts killed or missing. Jacobs page is first. A picture of his face half eaten off and a severely bruised body held onto his file with a paper clip.

“Did you tell Caps about this yet?” Mac asked with worry in his voice.

“No. I know they were close.”

“He trained him. Taught Caps everything.” Mac puts down the pictures, closes the file, and pushes it away from him. “What are you asking me to do?’

“Nothing.”

“Nothing?” Mac replies.

“Nothing at all. Don’t tell Caps anything. He’s good. Heck I’d even say he’s better than Jacob was at laying traps for the dead heads. But he’s disobedient and thinks too much. If he gets wind of this, he’s going to go out looking for revenge. And that’s the last thing. . .”

Mac cuts him off. “Revenge? You think who ever cleared out the hospital did this?”

Other officers in the room begin to chatter. Sal stands next to the projected image. He stares at it closely before responding.

“I never said that. Truth is I don’t know. Last we heard he was on the third floor on a building, off Victory Blvd. Said he saw something and wanted a better look. Next thing we heard is that his team found him on the ground level with tons of bruises and half a face."

"Who is on the rest of his team?"

"Those guys who got stuck on the Island when everything fell to shit. The pot head crew. I think their name was Brooklyn squad. They're now getting some R and R."

"Mind if I go ask them some questions? Maybe I could get some answers"

"Actually I do!" Sal said with a stronger tone in his voice. "Last thing I need is some investigation hampering any plans for defense. I already questioned them. They said they found him like that and that's it. Your job is to get some men in that radio tower and listen. Listen for anything. Is that clear?"

Mac just looks right back at his friend, his Commander. No answer comes from his voice. Commander Caladonato looks to the rest of the room and asks for some privacy. They all stand up, salute and walk out. He locks the door behind them. He then takes a seat right across from Mac and addresses him by his first name and says, "Mac. . . you're going to tell Caps, aren't you?" Mac nods yes.

"Ok well look tell him that's it's to find out who it is that attacked us. I don't want him disappearing for days like he usually does."

Mac rebuttals his argument. "He's gone for days because he brings back the most useful supplies."

Sal shakes his head, "I know. But we need to know where he is. We just lost our best scout. Can't afford to lose any more. You remember what he did to that rouge Woodrow crew? He fucking slaughtered them. Against orders."

Again, Mac rebuttals Sal's argument. "Two of them in that crew raped a 13 and 14-year-old girl. According to those poor things the rest held them down. Caps thought he was doing the right thing. Let's face it, we all knew what was going to happen to them"

Sal gets loud and hits the desk, "Yeah well it wasn't his call to kill them all! Seriously the guy is fucking nuts! He killed ten people in a crowded room all because they allegedly held down the two girls. Nobody fucking ordered him and Jacob to do that." Sal sensing tension building backs up, closes his eyes and rubs his temple to help with his headache caused by this argument. "We need order and law. When he goes off the rails, he causes wars. It's the only trait I wish he didn't pick up from Jacob."

Raising his hand to his forehead Sal thinks of the right words to say next.

"Pauline has been captured. I suspect its them. Whoever they are, they're going to get intel from her."

Mac starts shuffling through his paperwork again. Sal stops him.

"It just happened so you won't find a file on it just yet."

Mac looks up at his commander. "That's why you're brining up Caps. You're going to use him aren't you?"

Both of them stop talking and sit quietly for a moment. Sal walks over to the file cabinet and pulls out a cigar box and two small glasses. Walks back to the desk and hands Mac a glass.

"Thought you quit drinking?

"Yeah well I think we need one. Look I don't like this. Caps isn't military. He doesn't follow the chain of command the right way. But he listens to you. I would send someone else, heck I would even go, but I'm needed here to keep the peace. Tell him to get a team together and head out. If you do tell him, say it's so we can find out who did this. But do it discreetly. I need him to investigate. Ask questions and shoot later. Mission starts in the morning"

With that Sal opens the box and pulls out two small whiskey bottles. Using his teeth to open both bottles he pours the whole thing of each into each of the glasses.

Sal then toasts to their plan for their fallen comrades. "To revenge"

Mac reaches out with his glass "For Jacob".

Sal chokes on his drink. "Fuck I used to be hooked on this shit?"

Mac smiles and stops himself from laughing. When he stop's he asks, "So is Caps on his way back?"

"We got someone to pick him up. Another thing we found odd was the lack of dead heads in the area. It used to be flooded with them. Now not so much. Something big is coming Mac. I can feel it."

Mac puts down the glass and gives a half salute. "Sir, permission to address the men now?"

"Permission granted.

Home is not so sweet

Tow truck pulls up to the gate. The guards push open the doors quickly and the truck moves through onto the open grass.

Caps jumps out and runs to his room. Paige looks out the window to see what all the commotion is about. It's not often when vehicles are moving about due to the rationing of supplies and gas. When she sees Johnny running towards her direction, she quickly makes the bed and hides all the condom rappers. Lastly, she grabs the radio and heads towards the plant to hide it. Just then Johnny opens the door. Startled, Paige drops her radio next to the plant. It falls behind it. Johnny doesn't notice. He runs to the closet, pushes everything off a trunk and pulls it out by its side. Flipping open the top, Caps pulls out his weapon kit and starts pulling out belts of ammunition.

Paige seeing that it wasn't her that he was after asks, "What's going on? Your home so early"

"They got Pauline! Look I don't have time! I have to get more ammo." Caps pulls out a Uniform that Paige made for him. It has extra pockets to hold more rifle magazines. Its crudely put together. With some pockets being a different shade of blue than the cargo pants and shirt. But it works.

Caps starts changing his cloths as fast as he could. Paige looks in the direction of the plant and sees a small light in its shadow. The red power light shows its still on. She thinks to herself

Please don't call. Oh God please don't. Not now. At of all times, not now.

Caps calls on his ass when he tries to put back on his boots as fast as he can. Paige helps him back up. "Hey, sit for a min. What happened?"

"Fuckers ambushed us."

"Who?"

"No idea. They killed Sabrina. Pauline was taken away. I tried to kill them. The one fucking time I leave my rifle. FUCK! It was supposed to be a simple order drop"

Paige puts her hand over her mouth. Gasping she can't believe what she just heard.

"Ok well take a min to rest and-"

"WHAT? NO! I have to find her!"

Paige steps back scared. She's never seen him like this. Even when angry he's usually clear in thought, might even say something he realizes is wrong but apologizes soon after. But this is different. This is rage. Caps goes back to the trunk and looks down. He then turns around and says. “I’m sorry. Things were going according to plan and now they’re not. I have to go.”

Not saying a word Caps kisses her forehead and heads towards the door. Just as the door was about to close, he hears the faint voice with static.

“Hey Paige. He gone?”

Caps hearing this, pauses. Then opens back up the door. “What was that?”
Paige lies “I said good luck”

“That’s not what I heard”

Caps notices the direction she was facing. She was walking towards the plant when he was leaving. He looks in that direction and sees a red light. He walks towards it and Paige then rushes towards it. Caps was quicker and gets it before she does. He pulls out the radio from behind the plant and see Paige backing up.

Seeing her reaction Caps asks her one question. Shall we see who this is? She then says “It’s no one, just someone annoying”

Caps replies “Then can I call this person? I mean if its someone annoying then why is it a big deal for me to have this.”

He hand’s the radio back. “You’re not supposed to have this. So I’m giving you the option now come clean. Let me call him I want to hear it from whoever has the other radio.

Knowing she’s been caught she took a chance, hoping that her secret fuck buddy would keep his mouth shut, she hands back the radio

Caps presses the talk button “Who is this?”

The man on the other end of the radio replies back with the same words with a stereotypical Staten Island accent “Bro who is this?”

“This is Caps. Paige’s Boyfriend. Who is this?”

“The ex?

Caps then looks up at Paige in shock. “Who the fuck is this!”

“The names Frank. She talks allot of shit about you bro.”

Angry Caps doesn't realize he's holding down the talk button when he asks Paige if she slept with him.

When he lets go Frank answers for her.

"We fucked."

Paige then grabs the radio while its still in Caps hand. She pulls the hand holding the radio down to her, "No! Tell the truth! Just tell him the truth!"

"I just did." Frank says laughing

Letting go Caps then takes the radio back to where he can speak, "What proof you have? You have Pictures?"

"Yeah bro, but I'm not sharing shit with you."

Paige now tries to get the radio back. She hits Caps in the throat. Not realizing that it was an accident he restrains her arm's, so she doesn't get his again.

"WHY DID YOU DO THIS!" He shouts.

She screams "You're hurting me!"

Caps lets go. He wants to get hit her but can't bring himself to do it. He hands back the radio and demands she get her stuff. Without thinking he demands she leaves and never comes back. He also threatens to tell her mother what she did when he gets back. Paige stops near the door. “I’m not leaving till you say you won’t tell her.” Two others now walk by to see what was going on. She gets in his face. And starts hitting him while shouting “I did everything for you! You never show me how much I mean to you”

Refusing to leave and not wanting security to arrester her, Caps Picks her up and tries to bring her out of the makeshift apartment. She starts to throw punches. Caps lets go once she was outside. He then starts taking her stuff and throwing it out. Anger and hurt feelings are now taking place over rational thought. Paige tries to fight her way back in. Throwing punches at Caps. She lands one punch on his back when he wasn’t facing her. He doesn’t hit back but pushes her away. Not realizing his strength and forgetting Paige’s poor balance, Paige falls on her ass and rolls to her back.

One of the on lookers helped her back up as Caps loudly says “Fucking leave! You cheat on me while I was away!? With a fucking manipulating trash talker?! Never come back!”

Paige steps back as Caps slams the door. Shaking, she starts to walk away. She heads to her mothers.

Chapter 7

Communication is Key

Mac checks off all he supplies that Sergeant Darin Joseph and his squad are taking. Two fire teams loaded each and every pocket with 5.56 rounds. All carried M4 rifles. He then moves on to the second fire team near them.

One of the two fire teams was named Blue. This team consisted of Johnny Caps, Darin, the twins Greg and Rob and Joseph. The twins were selected for their knowledge of computers and radio equipment. They ran a Podcast before the world ended. Caps for this training in hunting and spotting by Jacob and a few other former military personal. And Joseph was there as support. All were comedians in their own right before the apocalypse.

“Broke out the good toys for us huh Mac?” Greg shouted to Mac. Rob came out of the building holding a shotgun that looked like something out of a cartoon.

“What on earth is that?” Greg shouted with excitement. Rob replied with “For duck season”.

The two then kept repeated the same phrases over and over again.

"Duck season"

"Rabbit season"

"Duck season"

Darin then jumps in "ENOUGH! Jesus fucking Christ will you just load up the truck!?" The two then start loading the truck with all the radio equipment and supplies near them. Whispering to each other the entire time Darin walks back to get more supplies.

"Duck season"

"Rabbit season"

Caps comes out with his own custom equipped rifle. An M4 with a red dot site and a scope that folds to the side. The barrel of the rifle was slightly larger than the standard that the others had. It had a fire grip as well, along with a bump stock.

He sits in the passenger seat. He doesn't try to hide the expression of anger on his face for having to come on this mission. Darin walks up to him. In an effort to provide comfort he tries to remind him of why he should come on this mission.

"Look, this will help us find her. If we can get that radio tower up and running, we can listen in and find out what they're planning and find out where she is"

Caps takes a deep breath, then turns his head to Darin and nods. Darin starts to walk in his direction but first looks at the twins and barks an order to move faster. As he does so, Caps reaches into his pocket and takes out a picture of him and Paige. Its them sitting on his bed. His head freshly shaven and his room freshly cleaned thanks to Paige. His anger starts to fade. He's reminded of how lucky he is to have found someone who cares so much about him after his father passed away. How she would do anything for him. He won't forget how everyone else abandoned him in his time of need. But she didn't. He flips over the picture and looks at the ring he has taped to the back. It's a two in one ring. One Dimond ring surrounded by the other. One goes to each of the couple that wears it. Below the tapped ring it has in his own writing.

I will make all the lost time I spent working up to you. All our hard work will pay off this summer. It all starts now. Will you marry me?

Within that paragraph there are some scribbled out sentences. He's been rewriting what to say how months. He puts the picture away in his hat and sees the other picture. It's of him with the rest of the comedy crew from Staten Island. The twins, Pat, Darin, Kushner, and Pauline. Caps anger then starts to boil in his stomach again. The events from the day prior still vivid to him. His breathing started to become heavy, his insides felt like they were a boil. He notices the blood stain on his brown boots. It was Sabrina's blood. Caps closes his eyes and tries to imagine something else. But all he can think about is how he failed at saving both of them. How he wasn't fast enough. Darin comes from the side and asks "You good? I heard you didn't even change your cloths from the last mission that you just started getting supplies together, then didn't even sleep. Look, I won't blame you if you wanna sit this one out." The sound of a door closing made them both jump.

It was Joseph. He let the screen door slam as he walked out of the building. He carries his M4 rifle, a pistol strapped to his leg, and Green nun chucks. The Twins looked at him as he got in the truck. Then looked at each other before turning back to Joseph before asking,

"Oh man, so. . . what's with the Nun chucks?"

"And why are they Green?"

Joseph just looks to them with glee in his eyes and says "These are my real Ninja Turtle nun chucks. I got them at comic con years ago. Been dying to try them out."

The Twins were dumbfounded by this.

"Let me just understand, what you just said exactly. Real. . . Ninja turtle. . . Nun chucks?"

Greg then chimes in. "Not fake plastic ones from like when we were kids?"

Both of the twins now say in unison "Real Ninja Turtle Nun Chucks?"

Joseph still not seeing the problem just replies with a "Yeah". The twins, Caps, and Darin just take a moment to stare at him.

The twins are the first to shrug off the use of his poor choice in weapons by responding with some sarcasm.

"Fuck it"

"Fuck it"

"He dies, then he dies"

Pointing at the logo on the nun chucks, Greg laughing says loudly, "He'll be ok. He's got turtle power"

Darin yells out one last time for everyone to get ready. He then walks back up to Caps. And puts his hand on his shoulder.

"Hey man you ok? I heard on the ride back to the base you kept blaming yourself."

Caps just keeps his head straight and doesn't reply.

"Keep your head in the game. We'll find her and get you back to your girl ok? Just no lone wolf shit on this mission."

Nodding his head, caps checks his rifle one last time before Darin starts the engine. The twins and Joseph sit in the back with ammo canisters by their feet. While waiting for the order to move out Darin orders everyone to check their weapons one last time.

Someone that none of the team has seen before walks through the door. He wore a white shirt with a union patch with the numbers faded away. He walked past Darin, not even acknowledging his existence. He walked as if he was on a mission.

He stopped in front of Johnny caps and asked, "You Johnny? Johnny caps?"

Replying with a nod Caps replies.

"I'm Frank Senior. Franks father. I came to apologize for my son. He's a bit of a fuck up."

Hearing those words Caps jumps from his seat. Frank Senior steps back and raises his open hands asking for Caps to stay calm."

“I didn’t come here to argue. I’m friends with a relative of your fathers. I just wanted to apologize. I know my son fucked up. I know your reputation. I knew your fathers as well.”

Seeing that the old man meant no harm Caps puts down his rifle but rolls up his sleeves in case Frank Senior says something he would regret.

“I know I really shouldn’t be asking you this but please just forgive and forget. He won’t talk to her again. I just got back from a small scavenger mission. I’ll go talk to him now. Just please don’t do anything till I get back. I know he talks allot just please ignore it for a day. Ok?”

Knowing that he can’t go see Paige anyways Caps reluctantly nods his head, agreeing to let him deal with it for now.

“Thank you. I’ll talk to you later after I speak with my son.”

As Frank Senior walked away Caps picked up his rifle and starred at him. Darin could see how upset he was. Turning around Caps can see he was being watched. It stopped him from making a rash decision. As he sat back down Caps thought to himself, *Ill deal with this later.*

Moments later Mac riding in a pickup truck with the other fire team pulls up next to Darin's truck and steps out. Gives a quick inspection of the supplies and says "Ok looks good. You guys know Brooklyn squad here. They will be helping you with this mission. Now to be clear one last time. Blue squad will be clearing out the buildings, Red will be outside moving from spot to spot around any building you guys clear out. Their job is to make sure no more get in and surprise you.

Mac walks around the truck one last time to shake Johnny Caps hand and give his sympathy's, "I'm sorry. I heard what happed between you and Paige" Mac pulls him in and tells him "Find em, do what it takes to get answers, then kill them all when you do".

Stepping back enough for both teams to see him he shouts, "I'll be here at base. Call back every fifteen minutes for a radio check till yawl reach CSI. Let's make this fast and clean people. You have your orders. Move out!"

Chapter 8

Information

The room was dark and hot with no windows. The only light that came in was from the space between the door and the floor. Pauline had been sitting there for hours. Her makeshift blindfold had come off while she rested. However, being tied to a chair, sitting up straight didn't allow her much. Her neck hurt from trying to rest her head on her shoulder. No food or water was brought to her. She was drenched in sweat. She wasn't escorted to any bathroom since the time she was brought there and had pissed herself. Her lips were dry and started to crack. She wore the same clothes from when she was first kidnapped. The smell was intense.

A noise could be heard. It was the sound of an echo. Boots clacking on the tile floor. But there was something else, a scratching sound. It was getting closer. Her mind raced with what it could be. A knife, an axe, Needles. *"Are n they going to drug me?"* She internally screamed. Suddenly the scratching noise stopped. Keys can now be heard shuffling. Pauline's heart rate began to rise as she heard the keys being put in the lock. She wanted to scream but knew it would do no good.

I needed to be stronger. She thought to herself.

The door unlocked. A moment passed that seemed to take forever. The door slammed open and two men who she guessed were over 6 feet tall rushed into the room and grabbed her by the shoulders and dragged her out of the room. She was facing forward; her feet being dragged next to the front two legs of the chair. She looked around as best she could. They didn't blind fold her, so she was free to look around. There are school projects on the walls. Turning right to a staircase, they went down to the first floor. Still being dragged, her feet got caught between the metal chair leg and the concrete step. Her pinky toe broke.

Another long hallway was in front of them. But they took a right into the gym and through the locker room. Once by the showers they put her down. One of the men pulled out a buzzer and started to take off her hair. Once buzzed they took off her hand cuffs and duct tape. One of the large men went to the locker next to them and pulled out a towel, some soap and cloths. Throwing them by her feet one of them says,

"Take a shower and get dressed."

Pauline looked at the sweats. They were marked by yellow paint. She turned around and started to unbuckle her belt. Not hearing the men walk away she paused, turned her head enough to see them, then asked “Some privacy?” They both crossed their arms and just stood there smirking. She turned back around and tried her best to ignore them as she took off her clothes. She kept the towel close by. The high windows shined a light that came right to the shower stalls. The water reflects the light and made the area around her look heavenly. It shined like a beam of light through the mist. Her light skin shined as the soap poured off her body. She took in the moment as a sign that everything will be alright. She closes her eyes and lets the water hit her face.

The moment was ruined when one of the guards walked over and shut off the water. “hurry up cunt” He said with an aggravated tone.

In defiance she turns back on the shower for a few seconds to wash the soap off. Pauline dries off quickly and puts on the clothes. The pants were too short, and the shirt was too big. She was given no socks but put her shoes on anyways. Handcuffed once she stood up she was then pulled by the chain connection her cuffs together. They went into the gymnasium.

A table was placed in the center of the room. Lots of canned food. Corn, beef, tuna, string beans, with a big fat turkey in the center.

“Do you like it?”

Pauline looks around and see An Elderly man with dark brown skin, silver fox hair, and matching goatee on the bleachers. The leader of the Brooklyn Knight’s approaches from behind. Pauline stands there in silence. She hasn’t seen a turkey in almost a year since the world ended.

“We found a few of these birds roaming around in the zoo. I was surprised as you are seeing it.” “They’re native to Staten Island correct?”

Pauline with no idea who this man is, watches as the old man walks towards the table with his wooden cane in his hand. He’s wearing a nice blue suite with three gold buttons. He pulls out a seat for Pauline. She hesitates. His smile is kind and inviting. He doesn’t wait for her to sit. Instead he walks over to his chair and sits down leaning his cane on the table.

“They’re native to Staten Island correct?”

She nods yes. “They were, deer too”

"Ah! We found one. But the infected got to it. We did manage to make the head into a trophy." He points above the door where Pauline walked in.

"You ever seen an infected animal before? I thought I did once. It was when I first came to your island. Whole family of racoons were infected."

It dawns on Pauline that she had never seen an infected animal before. All her time scouting, and not once did she see an animal turn into the nightmares that she sees when she closes her eyes at night. Her mother had turned. Her mother bit her father and he turned. She ran from them. Locked them in the house. The animals near her house, she never saw turn.

The old man smiles again. "Turns out it, was just rabies. Still scary, but also a relief". He then gestures to the food and says, "Please try it".

Pauline quickly responds, "Thanks but I'm full". The ruse she tried to pull falls apart immediately as her stomach gives out a large growl of hunger. The old man smiles before commenting, "You know, on average a person can last without food for about three, even four weeks. But water . . . a few days. Maybe a week if you're lucky. You though are very skinny. I suggest you eat something before the exchange"

"What exchange?" Pauline says with eagerness.

"My city is coming back to life. But such things take time. My men are clearing out the parts of Northern Staten Island as we speak. But such work isn't free. Your people have supplies. I made a list of everything we want and . . . "

"Want?"

"Yes, what I want."

"Not what you need? Just want is that it?"

Leaning back in his chair the old man realizes his mistake. His smile is now gone. "My apologies. I've been in charge for so long that I assumed you knew who I was. I guess my men haven't started their propaganda campaign yet. My name is Tyron Martinez. I'm the leader of the Brooklyn Knight's, I own the five boroughs."

Pauline looks at the man and without blinking says "Not ours"

Getting up from his chair without the use of his cane and with confidence in his voice Tyron stands and begins to slowly walk towards Pauline. “Now Before I start to make demands from your leaders for your exchange, I want you to tell me-”

“I’m not telling you shit!” She barks back.

“There won’t be any exchange. My boys are coming for me. You drew first blood. Up to this point there won’t be any negotiations.”

Tyron pauses. He sees a look in her eye that wasn’t there when she entered the room. He then turns around. Grabbing a grape off the table to eat on the way back to his seat. Sitting down he thinks for a moment. He stares at Pauline wondering what to say. Feeling a sense of defeat in the conversation he gets up to leave the room. Loudly he says as he’s walking towards the door “I have the best gangs of New York on my side. The Latin Kings, the Crypts, Bloods, even some Italian and Russians. Your people will come around and see-”

“We have the Marines! Army! Retired cops! Detectives! The best! You just have a bunch of drug dealers who run away in a fight! Even with my pants down to my ankles and taking a piss, I was able to knock one of your boys to the ground and still hit the others! We will kill every one of you!”

She flips over the table of food and throws a turkey wing at him. His guards quickly rush in and grab her by the arms, then hits the back of her knee, which makes her fall.

Being held in place she screams out one last thing. “We have enough supplies to last us years. We will keep fighting you forever if we have to!”

Tyron walks back, wiping off the skin of the turkey leg from his jacket as he strolls back in her direction. He takes his cane and places it under her chin to force her head up to look at him. Slightly leaning forward Tyron says with a smile, “Thank you. That’s all I needed to know”

Chapter 9

Red vs Blue

The way to the college was easy. Both fire teams felt confident since most of the dead are now just the slow-moving type. Still strong when they have you, but only able to walk, some walk in a brisk pace. There hasn't been a sighting of a Sprinter for months. Red team even had some fun on the route to the college. Two men used bludgeon weapons to see how many of the dead they could knock out. Both used golf clubs. Both were used while driving at high speed.

Pulling off of exit 8 and driving through the drop-down bar the two fire teams pull over in front of the campus. And coming under the underpass they see a body hanging. There's a sign around his neck. It says *Last will and testament in pocket.* Darin orders Mac to shoot at the rope so the body falls. Then orders caps to check out the body. Caps quickly runs over, pulls the note out and runs back.

"What's the note say? Rob asks.

"It's more of a suicide note than a will."

Greg is the first to respond. "Guess someone should have told him to hang in there"

Darin smiles, then drives away, continuing his route to the campus. Red team wasn't far behind them. In less than a few minutes the two fire teams came to the front gate of the college campus. Decaying bodies that are now almost fully decade to the point where only the bones and cloths remained were on the ground. Some got up and slowly lumbered to their trucks. Greg and Rob stood up in the back of the truck and used the roof as a makeshift bipod to hold their rifles steady. Each of them fired ten perfect head shots at less than a hundred yards. More were now coming from the woods. Caps counted and shouted that there were about thirty slow movers. Darin began to move his truck slowly through the open gate to keep the dead heads at a far enough but close enough distance to get accurate shots. Red team seeing this, began to fire wildly into the small horde of dead. The driver of red team even got out of his truck and started firing his shotgun. The horde was obliterated. All of blue team watches as red team cheered the dead's demise. Each of them fist pumping or giving each other high fives.

Mac shook his head and commented to Darin "These guys just waist ammo. Should we say something?"

Not missing an opportunity to roast a friend Darin replies, “Yeah, tell them to use your nun chucks next time.”

Mac sits back and sees everyone laughing. “Ok fuck you guys” And laughs with them.

Darin signals to red team to follow and keep a distance. He begins to drive slowly through the campus. Passing the old tennis court that was once surrounded by a bubble filled with air was now deflated. Some of the dead were clearly in there. Stuck but still moving towards the sound of the trucks. The building next to it was 1R. It housed the pool. The front doors were clear windows. A single body was holding up a door. When Darin pulled up closer, they could all see that it was only half a body. Mostly bone now.

Getting back on to the main road They could see building 1C. It housed the cafeteria and recreational rooms and the radio station on the opposite side.

Pulling up to the Entrance facing building 1R Darin shuts off the engine and pulls out his radio. First, he attempts to call Mac back at base. But no answer. Darin says to blue team “Looks like we’re on our own”. Darin waves his radio to red team.

“Red team come in”

“What’s up?”

“You guys pull up to the other side and make sure no dead come from there. Our boys will clear out this building”

“Roger”

With that order, red team drives to the other side of the building. Darin signals for everyone to get out and form a circle. “Ok boys, we’re here. Dead aren’t good at walking up or down stairs so let’s double time it to the staircase and clear out the top floor and work our way down. Caps you mentioned earlier that there’s only one staircase?”

“Only one in the center. Rest of them are emergency exits.”

“Ok that will work. Now let’s do this by the book. You guys remember the training that Kushner gave you right? Get into positions. Mac watch our six. Let’s do this swat style. Quick and clean. Got it?!”

With that order they move in. Moving though the two sets of clear doors and through the center lunchroom, each targeted a designated part of the circular room. Forming a 180-degree firing range. Desks and chairs were noticeably missing. Computers surrounding the lunchroom were broken. Glass was all over the floor in the room. Made staying silent all the harder. They cut straight through the middle of the room and to the staircase. Both entrances to the building had glass doors. Red team's truck was parked outside with no one in it. Rob is the one to point out that red team left their vehicle. "Where the fuck the go?" Darin signals to just keep moving up the stairs.

Carefully moving up the stairs and turning to the right they see the bookstore. It was barricaded in from the outside. Darin signals to turn around. "We'll check this out last he whispers"

Moving forward to the office rooms the small fire team gets ready to breach the door. They line up and with his left-hand extended outward for all to see Darin counts to three. He opens the door to the Auxiliary room, and they rush in. Each pointing their rifles at each's designated corner of the room. There was nothing. No bodies to see, no stench of death that lingered in the room. Nothing.

They moved on to the next room called the quiet room. This time Darin looked inside through the door window. Room was empty. All that was left was matts for resting. Darin turns to caps and asks "This is really a thing they had here? A quiet room? For resting?" Caps just shrugs his shoulders and nods.

Next was the student government office. Where one body was laying with its bottom half out the window. A bullet opening was in its skull.

Though seeing a dead body, blue team was not fazed. A year of fighting the dead had left them numb to the sight. Each room they went to clear out was the same.

The game room was the only one that showed them something different. Someone had taken some heads and put them in a triangle on the pool table. With one head on the opposite side acting as the white ball. Their bodies sat in chairs around the room. Some holding pool sticks. Three sat in the corner where there were gaming systems.

"This is fucked up" Mac said looking in the corner.

"Yeah. Whoever did this is setting us up." Darin replies as he grabs onto his radio.

Mac pushes over the bodies by the consoles and shouts, "No I mean look at this. Some asshole took a PlayStation controller and plugged it into the Xbox. Fucking monsters"

The whole fire team just pauses. Almost like they are trying to process what they just heard and what was going on in that room.

The lights suddenly turn on as does the TV and the consoles. The TV had its volume all the way up and echoed in the room and through the hallway.

Darin's training kicks in and Starts barking orders "LINE UP! We're leaving the way we came in! Move!"

Large growls can now be heard coming from down the hall. Instead of running from it, blue team moves towards it. Within no time they were back at the staircase. The noises were coming from the bookstore.

A blinking light was by the foot of the barricade. Darin quickly realizing what it was yelled "Get back now!"

The barricade blows up. Knocking both sets of double doors off their hinges. The shock of the explosion didn't do much. It was the shrapnel that did the most damage. The splinters from the chairs that held the doors closed hit Greg in his arm, shoulder, chest, and right hand. Mac was hit in the color bone with part of a metal chair leg. Rest of blue team was hit with fragments of chairs and desks as well but not as bad. Darin and Mac were the first to lift back up their rifles and point it towards the bookstore. Smoke and dust filled the air. The dead now walked and paced through the opening.

Darin shouted for everyone to fall back down the stairs and back to the truck. He gets on the radio and yells for red team to help. But no response. He tries again while jumping down the last few steps. Still nothing.

A sharp pain went through his leg. Falling to the ground he sees bullets bounce off tables and chairs around him. It was Red team. He saw two of them firing wildly with inaccuracy through the doors. Crawling to cover behind the wall near to avoid being shot he looked up and see the dead falling down the stairs. Caps was across from him, closer to the staircase. The twins and Mac were nowhere in site. But Darin sees the doors they came though earlier starting to close.

“They must have gotten out” He shouts to Caps. Caps points his rifle up and fires into the circular skylight. A body drops. It was one of red team.

“These fuckers betrayed us!” Caps shouts to Darin.

The herd of dead tumbled down the stairs. Pilling up on each other when they hit the bottom. By coincidence they created a barrier of flesh between blue and red teams. Giving Caps and Darin the opportunity to escape out the doors they came in. Running out the doors they see their truck. Its tires were popped and engine taken apart.

The dead were close behind. Tearing into the openings in the glass doors created by the rifle fire. More dead were outside with them, coming from the woods. The twins and Mac were gone as well.

Darin frustrated with the situation looks to caps and says “Fuck it! Let’s go on the offensive”

Running to the back towards the loading docks, the duo now attempts to outflank red team. The loading dock doors were closed and locked. The sound of rifle fire rang out briefly. At a brisk pace and rifles raised they continued around the building and came to the back doors of the radio station. The door was slightly open with bloody hand marks on it.

“Could be them” Caps whispers.

Darin slams open the door and they rush in. First room is the on-air control room. A body was laying down on the equipment. Its decaying body and dried blood all over the electronics.

“Clear”

Moving into the next room labeled News gathering, the Duo again finds nothing. Suddenly three shots were heard. Darin and Caps move fast down the hall, shoulder to shoulder, rifles pointed straight, they head into the waiting room. They see Mac on the floor choking one of the members of red team with his nun chucks. Another member of red team lays dead with a bullet wound to the head. Caps takes out his dagger and runs to help. He stabs the red team member through the bottom half of his jaw, stabbing the brain.

Darin ask’s “Where’s the twins?!”

Rob shouts from the room labeled Music library. “In here” Mac then pushes the body off of him, Caps helps him up.

“I’m fine by the way” Jams says sarcastically as he gets up and locks the door in the waiting room.

Darin sees the twins pointing their rifles at the last two of red team. They had their hands up. Each were in a separate isle in the room. They could see each other through the gaps in the moveable shelves. One was bleeding from his gut. He was slashed three times. Rob lost his rifle in the fight. He held his pistol in one hand and knife in the other. Greg held his rifle up as best he could. The splinters in his arms went in deep. One of which was as big as a finger.

"What we got here?"

Rob answers "Found these two destroying out truck. Took off when we started shooting. Dumb asses left their rifles on the floor when they were doing that. Started running back to their boyfriends here when we started shooting"

Darin looks to Greg and asks if he's ok. Greg just nods his head. His mouth was swollen. One of his front teeth was now broken in half. It hurt to talk.

Looking back towards the captives, Darin shouts out to Mac to lock the back doors. He then takes a knee in front of the bigger of the two captives. He patted him down and pulled out a doorag. It was the colors of the Latin Kings with another flag sown on the back of it. It was a silverfish background with a laurel wreath crown. Some of the leaf's had symbols of gangs and some of the boroughs.

"Guessing this is the flag you guys are using huh?"

The captive doesn't say anything. He just stares back at him. His dark brown eyes and unibrow make for a scary sight. He looked incredibly strong. And his tattoos made for a terrifying sight. If standing, he would tower over everyone in Blues fire team. His black skin blended in the with the dark room.

Looking back to Rob, Darin asks “How did you take them down?”

“You only got me cause this boy is a pussy!” The Latin King shouted when looking back at his comrade through the opening on the shelf.

Darin looks back and checks out the other captive. Patting him down, he notices something sticking out of his back pocket. He pulls out a similar doorag This time it was that of the gang called the Bloods with the same laurel wreath crown on the opposite side. The captive didn’t look up. But Darin recognized him from around camp. He was once the cook back at the camp before they took the prison. His sleeveless shirt exposed what he was before the world ended. Cut and needle marks showed his past addiction.

Caps walks into the room. “They say anything?” Darin shakes his head no. He now walks past Darin and up to the Latin king. Squatting down to be at eye level he says to the Latin king, “You wanna talk there buddy?” He says nothing. Stepping back Caps notices that the Blood gang member is now looking up at him. Quickly Caps aims and fires his rifle and switches it to full auto. One of the bullets hits the Latin King's main artery in this throat. Blood now squirts and sprays through the opening in the shelf, hitting his comrade on the side of his face. The old Blood member's face has the look of shock. Wetting his pants, he starts reciting prayers.

Darin pulls Caps by the arm "You know what you're doing?"

He responds back "Just following orders"

Crouching down to be at eye level with the blood, Caps uses his knife to lift up his head so he's looking at him. "You know my reputation. What I like to do to evil people like yourself?"

No response. Just blank stares.

"Well let me refresh your memory."

Caps grabs him by the hair and holds his head down. Using his knife, he slices off the Blood's left ear. When the Blood tries to stop him, Caps grabs his hand, puts it on the lower end of the shelf and stabs it, pinning the Blood to the shelf.

Screaming in pain, the Blood then starts to recite prayers once again.

"Look at me asshole! Your friends have one of our friends. And you're going to tell me where they're keeping her. Or I'M going to have fun with you."

The Blood doesn't respond. He just keeps praying. Switching between broken English and Spanish. Caps hands his weapons to Darin.

Grabbing the blood by his head with both hands he looks him in the eyes, "I know you understand me. I'm in no mood to fuck around right now. So, you're going to start talking or I'm going to show you what slicing techniques I learned while working in the deli as a kid. You got it?"

The Blood looks back with tears in his eyes. "I didn't want to do this"

Whispering back, "Shh, shh, shh, shh. I don't care. Because now, you're going to do what I say. And I say tell me everything. Got it?"

Chapter 10

Talking things out

Mac leaning on the guard rail, sips from his coffee. He walks out of the makeshift tower that some of the engineers built on top of the abandoned fuel oil tanks. Graffiti surrounded both of them. No one dared painted over the art work. It was old but good. Almost like looking back in time.

He took a minute to observe John Kuschner's training. Kuschner was the new instructor for these recruits. A former softball captain and electrician, he was a good asset to have as an instructor. Today was Cardio followed by classes in how to hot wire a car. Once all thirty people were in formation Kushner opened up with a joke, he told Mac earlier.

"You're all probably wondering what part of the body we will work out first and how to determine that! Well jump up and down a few times. . . and whatever jiggles the most is what we'll work on this day."

Mac leaning on the guard rail can't help but laugh when he sees the recruits checking to see what part of their bodies jiggle. The civilian corps starts doing jumping jacks and counted in cadence with Kuschner.

"ONE! TWO! THREE!"

"ONE!"

"ONE! TWO! THREE!"

"TWO!"

Some of the dead nearby walked towards the sound of the counting. Men with makeshift spears waiting behind the gates of the prison, ready to stab at them when they got close.

Mac checks his watch. He notices the time that went past since Darin last checked in

Darin hasn't called in for 30 minutes. Better send someone to check on them.

Just then Darin's voice comes in on the radio.

"This is blue team! We're coming to the gate. ETA five minutes. Have a medical team ready!"

The stress in Darin's voice is showing as he speaks.

"Is anyone getting this!"

Mac answers "We hear you loud and clear." Mac orders the guards at the gates to stand ready. He then sends one of the guards to order Kuschner to bring everyone inside.

Last thing he wanted was for people to panic at whatever it is the fire teams were running from.

Looking through his binoculars, Mac looks out towards the highway. He only sees one truck. But there's six people in it. Not five.

Handing the binoculars over to a watch tower guard, he then starts running down the stairs. Once at his SUV he noticed a dead head crawling towards him. Instead of stabbing the struggling biter, Mac started his engine and ran the dead heads head.

Reaching the front gate at the same time as Blue team, Mac can see who the sixth person is. It was one of red team. From what Mac can tell he was bleeding badly from his head.

Once past the front gate, Darin drives to the medical bay. They all get out and help the Blood inside. Mac follows close behind. He tells Darin to come to his office right away for a full report.

"You guys stay here till the guards arrive to relieve you. Watch him till then. Rob get yourself fixed up. . . Where's Caps? Never mind. I know where he went."

As Darin went back with Mac for a briefing. Caps went back to his apartment.

As he opened his door he looked around. He dared not call out her name. Everything was the same. Only a few things were missing. A poster drawing from the movie Alien, some plush pillows shaped of teeth that Caps had gotten Paige for her birthday. But most notably, her voice. She was always there to greet him when he came back home from a mission.

Standing in the middle of the room, with his bed to the right and kitchen to the left, he tries to think of what to do next. Usually he had a gift that he brings back for her. His routine is broken.

Covered in dirt, blood, and broken glass, he starts taking off his clothes on the way to the closet, not caring about the mess he left behind. None of Paige's cloths are there. All space was shared between them. All the empty space hurt to look at. She always organized his clothes by color. He took out Dark brown cargo pants, underwear, socks, and a brown and black shirt.

He also takes out a towel and one of the jugs of water. After pouring some water on the towel, he starts to wipe off the dry blood from his body. He knows he should be having some sort of flashback of the awful things he just did. Or of the fights he had. But the only thing he could think about, was her. He wondered if she was ok.

Thoughts of what to say to her raced through his mind.

What do you say after what she did? After what I did? Do you apologize to someone who cheated on you? He thought to himself.

Washed and dressed Caps looked around one more time. A sort of muscle memory kicked in. Whenever he got dressed, he would be hugged from behind from her. This time there was nothing which made him feel uneasy. More questions filled his head. *What did I do that made her cheat? What didn't I do that made her unhappy?*

Not one to sit and dwell on this without answers, he put on his boots and locked the door behind him. He started walking to the one place she would be. The one place he dreaded and feared the most in an apolitical world. Not some ex's or even to the man she cheated on him with apartment, not to the interrogation room. But to the one place he wanted never to see. . . her mothers.

While walking towards his ex-girlfriends' mothers apartment he thought of what to say. But nothing felt right. *Do I ask to see her?*

What if she says no? Do I just demand answers?

He came to her door. It was red with drawings on the bottom. All were from her little cousins. He recognized the artwork. They often drew pictures of the family. Each of the males had a Yakama on. All the females had blond hair.

Caps knocked twice. No answer. Knocking again he heard something fall over inside.

"Paige, that you? Look I just want to talk"

The door slightly opens with the chain lock on. Her mother Lisa opens up. "She doesn't want to talk to you. You hurt her."

"What?! No. . . not intentionally. She hit me. I didn't hit her. She was caught cheating on me with that weirdo Frank. Look I just wanna-"

Cutting him off in mid-sentence Lisa snaps. She yells so everyone can hear her.

"Enough! You hurt her! She didn't cheat! My daughter would never do that! And if she did that means something was lacking in the relationship. You should have talked it out when you found out. Now! Leave! Or I'm calling security!"

Just as Caps was going to respond, Lisa slams the door. Biting his lip so as not to start cursing at his ex's mother, Caps turns towards his apartment and starts walking back. Kicking over an empty crate along the way.

Turning the corner, he sees Commander Caladonato with three security officers. They also see him.

"Look I left ok. I'll kick the shit out of Frank on my own time. No need for you to watch over me."

The security officers surround caps. "Mind telling me why you tortured a prisoner? And who the fuck is Frank?" Sal asks.

"He's the guy who manipulated my girl. As for torture, I'm not sure what you're talking about. He fought and lost to us. You set us up with a bunch of people you knew would betray us."

Sal shakes his head. "No, that wasn't my intent. I just didn't believe it at first. Go do what you came here to do. Kick his ass, then come to the office."

Sal and his guards walk past Caps and down the hall. Before turning the corner, Caps asks loudly “Wait did you just give me permission to kick the shit out of someone?”

Sal answers back with some sarcasm in his voice and repeats some of what Caps just told him. “I’m not sure what you’re talking about, but when you’re done come see me. I have new orders for you”

Now with permission to let out some frustration Caps heads back to Paige’s mother’s apartment. He knocks three times and demands to know where Frank is. There’s no answer. He knocks again, this time the door opens. The room is almost empty. Only things left in the place was the couch with patches of different colors sown into it, cardboard boxes, and some garbage is left behind. Heading to the couch first to see if some spare keys were left behind by accident, Caps lifts up the couch cushions, but only finds an old granola bar. Next, he checks the trash. Ripping the bag from the top he then slowly starts dumping its contents on the floor. Looking for any paperwork that might tell where Frank lives. Nothing was there.

Feeling at a loss Caps gives up. Wipes his hands on the couch in an attempt to clean his hands. Putting back the cushions he sits down on the couch and opens up the granola bar. Seeing that the chocolate is white he throws it at the trash. Caps sat there for a moment. Pondering what to do next. That's when he sees it. A small envelope with the numbers 88 on it. No name. Just a number on a white envelope with lipstick where it's supposed to be sealed.

They didn't move into his place. . . did they? Caps thought to himself. Room 88 was close by. Realization kicked in on how he never saw this coming. Frank lived close by. Caps room was 66.

Caps runs out the door towards franks apartment. Soon its right in front of him. Turning his shoulder towards the door and running at full speed, Caps breaks open the door and lands sideways into the room. Getting up quickly he screams for Frank to come out. But no one is there. Again, Caps finds an empty room. Just some furniture is left behind. But one thing stuck out. A sticker on the dresser mirror. It was a pink letter P. In small letters on the bottom it said Paige was here. This was the same notice that he got when Paige used to put on his door when she showed up unannounced at his house. At first Caps smiled at the memory. He remembered how he loved little surprises like that. How before the apocalypse every moment like that was cherished.

Right above the P is a quote. It reads 'Life is made of small moments like this'. It wasn't written in her handwriting. Caps' blood felt as if it was boiling. Reason and understanding was replaced by anger and rage. He stares at his own reflection. Suddenly grabbing the mirror by its side with his left hand, he starts punching his reflection with his right. Over and over again his fist aims for his own face. Shouting as he does so, "How did you not see this! Mother fucking cunt! Son of bitch! Ahhhhhhhhhhh!"

Caps throws the mirror to the ground with his left hand and lets out one last scream. His voice echoes down the hall. One old lady opens her door to see what's happening. She sees him with his bloody hand, she locks eyes with him. Startled, the old lady jumps back, slamming her door shut as she does so.

Caps falls to the ground. Looking down at his hands, he sees that his shaking, shards of glass in his knuckles. Putting them down he sees his reflection in the broken pieces of the mirror.

"Fuck her. Fuck him too. Screw orders. He's a dead man." Caps says to himself.

Finding a washcloth near the sink, Caps cleans his hands and walks out the apartment.

The plot thickens

Sal Mac, and some officers sit quietly in the office. Outside of the office Darin and blue team wait as each of them are interviewed one by one. Sal's secretary is in the room recording what Blue team is telling them about the events that took place. All of them are honest. Caps was the last.

"I already heard what you guys went through."

"So, am I free to go?"

Sal notices the bandages around his knuckles and asks. "Please tell me that's from you hitting Frank and not your ex"

"Whoaaaa!" Caps is taken back by the comment.

"I didn't hit her."

Sal pulls out a yellow envelope from his bag, and slides it across the table.

"Looks like she has some bruises on her forearms. Mind explaining that?"

Caps looks at the photos, then looks back up at Sal with an expression of distaste.

"I grabbed her. So what? Not like I hit her. Sure as hell wasn't going to let her hit me again. I'm a pretty strong guy. If I did hit her she would be in a comma right now."

Sal looks to Mac, then looks back to Caps and replies, "Agreed, but that said she's been moved. Going to our Northern base.

"And Frank?"

Both Sal and Mac get up, each walk around the table from opposite sides. Caps knowing he's being surrounded quickly stands up. Sal and Mac sit down in front of Caps. Sal talks first. Trying his best to escalate the situation he talks as calmly as he can.

"He's with her."

"What!?"

"I wish I could say it didn't get worse"

Demanding more answers in a louder tone, Caps steps forward and gets in Macs face, "What the fuck you mean worse!?"

Holding his arms up slightly and holding Caps by the shoulders, Mac tries to calm him down. Sal steps in and briefs Caps on what happened. "They went to our northern outpost near the ferry. From there we learned the guy Frank was the reason why Pauline was captured. When you told Paige about the orders, she told him. He then relayed the info somehow to the enemy.

"You're lying!" Caps screams while pointing his finger. Mac holds him back.

Sal picks up the envelope from the table and opens it. He pulls out a small book and hands it to Caps. To show that he's not the enemy Sal refers to Caps by his first name.

"Johnny, look at this."

The cover and sides had blood on it. The corner of the cover was torn. Caps opens it to the page with a sticky note in it. It shows details of supplies, troop movements, and details of places where Caps had been in the past month. Turning a few pages back he noticed Paige's name written. Sal tries to take back the book, but Caps moves away.

"You don't want to read that"

Caps keep reading. Frank's handwriting is bad but he can make out that he was manipulating her. He was planning on what to say to her when Caps was going on scavenging and scouting missions. Plans on how Frank would convince Paige on that Caps didn't care about her, how to make it seem like he didn't appreciate her. On the top it two words were underlined with a wavy line. Operation doubt.

"I don't understand" He says closing the book.

"Looks like either Paige was in on this operations or Frank was using her for info. Not just to get some pussy. He's a first-class manipulator. He targeted her since she was in charge of our supply inventory. Must have been here since. . ."

Stopping Sal in mid-sentence Caps asks "No, why tell me this?"

Sal opens the envelope again. He pulls out pictures. Handing them over to caps and takes back the book with some force. Then asks for him to sit.

Taking a seat and shuffling through the photos Caps sees the carnage. The forward outpost was a disaster.

"Ten of our troopers were killed. Four are missing. Paige, her mother, Frank, and his father."

Mac then puts his hand on his shoulder to tell him the last bit of bad news. It was something he didn't want to tell him.

"Jacob is dead as well. We suspect that it was that it was red team since they just betrayed us."

"Let me guess, Paige and Frank knew about that too?" Caps asks while his hand gripped into a fist.

Sal tries to divert the anger he's seeing within his friend.

"I don't think so. Nothing in Frank's notes indicates that. I think you need to let her go. We got bigger things to worry about."

Loosening his fist, Caps nods his head in agreement with Sal. Standing up and stepping back against the wall he closes his eyes and takes a deep breath to try and relax.

"Why don't you go back to your apartment? Rest for a bit. We're weighing our options to see how to deal with this situation. We need to come up with a plan to get Pauline back. But we can't do that with you acting like a psychopath."

As Caps walks to the door Sal stops him to ask one final question.

"Hey one thing we couldn't get. Did our captive ever tell you how he did it? How he arranged those bodies. The ones in the game room."

With one foot out the door, looking back Caps replies, "He didn't. That guy acted like he had no idea what I was talking about. And I tortured that guy for at least an hour. I don't think he would lie about that."

As the door closed and Caps left. Sal and Mac looked at each other. Both had more questions now than answers.

If you won't then I will

The next morning Mac sent Mac to get Caps to report to newly established war room. Mac had requested for Caps to report to him over an hour ago. But got no response on the radio. Everyone in the room was waiting patiently. Sal just stared at the maps. Jotting what hills to hold and chock points. Squad leaders that lived in some areas of interest would be asked to give details about the terrane so as to plan ambushes.

Radio chatter filled the airwaves as outpost after outpost fell to the Brooklyn Knights.

One squad leader pulled Commander Caladonato over to ask what to do about their situation.

"Sir, should we try to negotiate our surrender? Herds of slow walkers we can take on. Heck even those infected sprinters I'll fight. But we can't hold out against. . ."

Commander Caladonato cuts him off and pokes his finger into the man's chest.

"Don't ever say that shit to me again. Got it!?"

The man steps back and takes his seat. Commander Caladonato goes back to his paperwork. He formulated a plan to take back one outpost by the bridge, hoping to cut off some of the Brooklyn Knight's supply chain. It worked for about an hour, but the Knight's sent in reinforcements. Sal ordered his men to fall back to close-set exit near the Verrazano and Fingerboard road. Ordered his men to hold out on the overpass and the buildings a Jasion to it. All other units were to burn all areas between them and the enemy. The plan was to buy time while harassing the enemy.

Mac entered the room and handed a note to Mac. It was from Caps. It reads,

Sal, I'm sorry but I'm leaving. I'll find both Pauline and Paige on my own. You guys fight conventionally. It's taking a toll on us. Jacob taught me that sometimes you need to do some hellish things to get into heaven. I'll do what I can to clear a path if they get in my way. I can't work if I have to wait for orders. I'm taking one car and some ammunition.

Commander Caladonato looked at the note next then asked Mac if he had any idea of where he might be heading. Just then one of the scouts said on the radio shouted that a group was attacking an outpost belonging to the Brooklyn Knights. Sal, Mac and some of the other squad leaders listened and waited.

Moments later the scout reported in.

“Sir the area has been wiped out. 25 enemy KIA. Hey wait. There’s a note. It says ‘Welcome to the quiet borough’, Sir, we have no men nearby to take and hold this sector. should I leave it for the enemy?”

Mac ordered “Yes. Leave some traps there as well.”

“Roger that.”

Chapter 11

Betrayed by all

Earlier while Caps was away

Laying down in the truck Paige, tried to shut her eyes and calm down. It wasn't the potholes the truck kept running over that was keeping her awake. It was her anxiety. She was angry, sad, and filled with regret. Her mother's lap provided some comfort for her head.

Laying down she turned to her side and felt like something was stabbing her in the neck. Leaning forward she noticed her chain was twisting and the Star of David was poking her. Unlocking the clamp, Paige holds up the white gold chain, so the star is above her head. As the chain dangled in the air and unwinds itself, thoughts of her ex came to mind. *He took it off a dead head. Risked his life for her.* At the time she didn't think much of it. *This was something he did every day.* She thought to herself.

At first thoughts of the arguments they had come to mind. *How dumb they were*, she thought. Then thoughts of what they did for each other came to mind. On how he introduced her to his friends, how he took her everywhere. How he always tried to make her laugh, how he brought her to comedy clubs and parties and always introduced her to people. She remembered the corny lines he would say about comedy "The best comics are those that can put fun in funeral" Some of the best memories was how Caps always seemed so proud and happy to call her his. The biggest was how Caps introduced her to his family and friends. How much that meant to him since he had so few left. Thoughts of his house and how much they worked on it after Johnny's Caps father died. She remembered the talks about how he wanted her to move in. How things were getting better. How he never used the words for HIM, but always said that things were getting better for US. It was then that she realized that he did appreciate her.

That was of course before the world ended. It was then that he was too busy.

Putting the necklace away in her pocket, Paige turns to her side and looks at Frank sitting next to his father. He has heavy eyelids and a receding hair line that he tries to hide by combing his hair forward. Not very good at talking but she liked him since he was there and listened to her. When they smoked weed together, she felt a connection with him. When weighing that last thought against the things her ex did, doubt came to mind. *Did I feel something for him or was it just the weed? Was*

I not feeling the same way about my ex anymore since I slept with a few people? Was I forcing myself to forget the good things about him for what I did?

Realization came to her. That the time for thoughts like these no longer mattered. She was with Frank now. Any regrets she had didn't matter. Paige sat up, took her necklace out and threw it out the window. While in midair Moon light reflected off the diamonds that rested within the star. It shined in her eyes for a brief second. Feeling emotional she opened her backpack and pulled out a flask filled with Jack Daniels. Taking she poured a shot but spilled most of it due to the bumpy road. Paige poured a second one. But that too spilled. Fed up with the road, she takes one last long swig straight from the bottle. She lays her head back down on her mother's lap.

Not long after they arrived at the outpost. It was the only house they cleared out in the area. All the others were still infested with the dead. Most of whom by now were the slow type. It oversaw Hero park and had a clear line of site down victory road. Looking North, you could see the lower end of Manhattan.

This spot was perfect. Houses nearby had lawns that were on a hill and stone walls.

Clove Lake Park was close by. It had helped stop the dead as well. It was an open area where the grounds incline would bring rain water into the lake. That same angle made it hard for the dead to come out of the park. Its lake had a water filtration system built in the center. It sat on a stone bridge that people used for crossing. Center of the bridge had two stone towers that held the filers and bathrooms for guests. Sometimes the dead would get stuck in the lake and never get out. Victory road itself was a deterrent as well. It was steep and the dead have always had trouble on hills. Dead heads may never get tired, but they are clumsy.

Getting off the truck Paige and her mother struggled with their luggage. Frank just walked right passed them. He clearly saw she wanted some help but was ignored.

“Thanks’ a lot!” She said loud and sarcastically.

Frank, seeing he’s being a bit rude, walks back, “Oh right sorry. Mind is elsewhere right now”

Shoving her mom aside to grab the smallest of the bags he excuses himself by saying in his strong Staten island accent “sorry bro”

Besides how much of a jerk Frank was being she noticed that he packed light. Not much clothes or food. When she asked about it he just shrugged it off.

They stayed in their room while others unpacked. Spending their time smoking weed and fucking. Lying in bed, she noticed that Frank didn't sleep well. She tried to spoon with him, but he complained it was too hot. A thought of something Caps did came to mind. She started to miss how he would hold her close and say "Mine". How he would hold her close and kiss her.

Later on that night when trying to sleep Paige noticed that Frank kept getting up to look out the windows.

"Stop being paranoid and come back to bed."

"Going for a quick walk."

To where? We can't leave at night without back up. You. . . "

"YO! Get off my back!" He snaps back in frustration.

He grabs his flair gun from his bag and walks out into the back yard. Looking at his watch he seems to be waiting. Paige watches as he fires the gun into the air. A red burning flame lights up the sky. It was 8pm.

Half an hour later after smoking more weed Frank started asking more questions about the supplies back at the headquarters.

"Do you remember how much food we had to last us? How much ammunition we had?"

Paige started to get a weird feeling about him. He seemed to only be flirty when asking about home base.

The sound of a seemed like a car back firing was heard right outside their window.

"What was that?"

Frank then tells her to get under the bed with him. That everything was going according to plan.

"What plan? What the hell are you talking about?"

Gun fire was now heard all around them. People that were their friends screamed in pain. Paige tried to get up but Frank grabbed her.

"Nothing you can do now" He shouted.

"We'll be ok"

The gun fire stopped. A voice in the distance yelled out “Flash” In response Frank yelled back “Thunder!”. Paige then yelled out “What the fuck is going on?!”

The door opens and in comes two men who grab Paige by the arms and lift her to her feet. “Come with us”. Walking into the living room Franks father sat on the couch. Paige’s mother was laying on the floor. She was shot in the stomach. Paige ran over to her.

“One of you guys help!” She shouted.

A man walked in from behind. A tanned skinned bald man with a Camouflage jacket and ginny tee walks into the room with two others. “This her?” He asks Frank.

Replying with a nervous lump in his voice, Frank says, “Yes Louie. . . I mean Sir”

Louie signals for the other men in the room to take Paige’s mother to the truck outside. Paige sat there on her knees, shaking, with tears running down her face, unable to move. Louie walks up to her and takes a knee and lifts her face up by her chin, he was going to say something but Paige talked first.

“I’ll do what you want, just please help her.”

With that out of the way, Louie signals with one hand for everyone to round up and head out. Frank walks past her.

"You did this? Why?" Paige asks.

Stopping at the door Frank turns around and takes two steps back in her direction. Being as blunt as he can he replies.

"It's nothing personal. I used to sell weed for these guys. Well some of them at least. If anything, I did you a favor. Staten Island is going to fall. These guys are the badest of the bad. If they can survive the dead coming to life, then they deserve the supplies we have at the prison."

More tears run down her face. "You used me? How could you manipulate me like this?"

Smiling at Paige, Frank couldn't help but feel like he needed to explain how he wasn't the bad guy.

"You wanted this! You told me he didn't appreciate you. Now I know that wasn't true. All the things he did for you, all the people he introduced you to, and the things he gave you, I just played to what was immediately bothering you. Your friends didn't even like him and most of them never met him. So, face it girl, you wanted something new. He was out working hard for a good future with you, but I offered you a good immediate time. You chose this!"

Wiping away her tears, Paige starts to stand up. Her foot was numb from the way she was sitting. But she wanted to show some strength, so she kept walking towards the door. But Frank stopped her.

"If you think you're going to go back it's too late. It takes a whole lot to forgive someone for cheating. Your man isn't up for it. My father talked to him on the way out. He threatened my father. Not that I care, he's going to die soon anyways."

Paige looks back at him "He really threatened your father?"

Smiling back Frank knows he has her. But decides to tell the truth. "Na, but they did talk though. Looks you're one of us now. Like I mentioned before, your friends didn't even like him. Weird seeing how they didn't even know him, anyways I asked the big man to spare them as well. So you'll be-"

Paige slaps him in the face to get him to shut up.

Touching his lip, Frank notices he's bleeding. "I'll wait for you downstairs. Don't be long."

Watching Frank walk down the stairs, through Hero park, her mind raced of what had just occurred. She betrayed someone she connected with for a man who tricked her. She ran to the truck where her mother was being kept and road with her to the Brooklyn Knights base. Two men were with her. One was wearing an old EMT jacket. She looked to her mother, trying to comfort her she said, "Look see? You're going to be ok". As the two men controlled the bleeding, Paige held her mother's hand. She held it the entire trip.

Soon after

The ride took almost two hours. Crossing the Verrazano was quick. Paige saw how the Brooklyn Knights were attacking all the small outposts round the Staten Island side. When it came to the dead, they mostly used bladed weapons instead of firearms.

Soon after they were riding along the Belt pkwy. No dead were there. The highway was above ground and above buildings so no dead could reach them. All the cars pulled off the final exit before tunnel and into Brooklyn Heights. They passed roadblock after roadblock. Paige looked out her window at each roadblock so see why they stopped. When asked what business they had showing up, Louie would use a hand signal to show their intentions. Though unable to make out what the hand signal fully described Paige was able to tell that hand signals were gang signs.

When they finally stopped two guards opened the back of the van and carried Paige's mother on a stretcher. Trying to hold her hand on the way inside Louie pulls her by the arm.

"Come with me. The main man wants to speak with you and Frank."

"I want to see where my mother is going!" She screams.

"Relax honey. She'll be alright. I saw the wound. Went in and out. No vital organs were hit."

Frank tries to help get Paige to calm down.

"Don't worry bro, let me handle this. Paige just do as they say. We can smoke after. You Ma will be alright. Don't worry baby."

With a boom in her voice she yells "FUCK YOU!" and smacks Frank across the face again.

Frank steps towards her aggressively with closed fist. But Louie stops him and orders for him to meet them there. When Louie turns around, he suddenly gets an order to stand down from a shadowy figure who stood next to the wall. It was one of the few areas with no light. When he steps closer Paige could see that he was large man with a receding hair line, with the rest of his remaining hair slicked back. His teeth are a yellowish color.

"Now honey that wasn't very nice. Still I like you. Why don't you and I chat first and tell you how things get done around here?"

Then the man looks to Louie and says "You are relieved good sir"

She follows him to the church. Walking past the confessional and into the back room, there's a kitchen. He throws her an apple and tells her to eat and sit down.

As she sat and ate the man introduced himself and described the rules that she would have to follow.

"I'm Michael. Now baby. You need to know your place. See we are a very generous organization. We treat our friends very, very good." He says with a wink and a smirk.

As he paused in his speech he slowly walked around the room. Almost as if he was inspecting it. Then continues.

"See Women here are safe when they are with me. I treat them with lots of . . . pleasurable memories."

Talking and walking, Paige listened. She was about to take a bite of the apple when she noticed a small hole in it. It was dripping as well. Suspecting it was drugged she put down the apple.

"I'm not very hungry" She said.

Pausing once again and realizing he wasn't going to get her drugged he slowly walked up behind her. Leaning over he smelled her hair and began to rub her shoulders.

"You must be stressed out. Why don't you let me help release some tension?"

Going for a kiss on the neck Paige quickly stands up and backs away. She tried to put some distance between them. But he just kept getting closer.

"Get the FUCK way from be you Bill Cosby wanna be!"

"Enough!

Michael turns to see Tyron Standing in the doorway with two of the biggest body guards he's ever seen. Both had a pistol on their hip and a baton in their hand.

With a fake smile Michael tries to play off what he was about to do. "Sir! I was just about to. . ."

"Get out" Tyron yelled.

Michael moves at quick speed to leave the room. Tyron gives him one last command before he does.

"I want all information that you have gathered on my desk in fifteen minutes.

As Michael then runs to the nearest office to begin typing up a report, Tyron offers Paige a seat and throws away the dripping apple.

"Well looks like we are off to a rough start. My apologies for what has happened. Michael is. . . a very lonely man. Can't separate his work from personal life."

"Is my mother ok?"

"She's fine. I'll take you to see her after you tell me everything you know about the Prison. Frank says you were the management supervisor for all provisions. That you tracked everything that went in and out. Is that true?"

Paige just looks back at him and stares. She doesn't know what to do. She watches his reactions. He's an old man. Not strong looking but clearly is in charge. Looking him up and down she also can't help but feel impressed by the man's tailored suit. He dressed like a gangster from old 50s movies. Not like the losers she saw outside. He had a cane with a gold trim and fedora hat. On the side of the fedora was a symbol, a laurel wreath crown. Same symbol was also in the pocket handkerchief in his suits front pocket.

Tyrone snaps his fingers twice and the guards start putting out dishes and a meal for them to eat. One opens a bottle of red wine. As they do so Tyron tries to keep the conversation going.

"You went through a traumatic event. I understand why you might be. . . reluctant to tell me anything."

Paige continues to listen and be amazed at what she was seeing. These giants of men were obeying orders without question. Not out fear but out of respect. Back home if Sal gave an order to a civilian often why would ask "but why" instead of just doing what was told.

Within a few minutes two personal pizzas were made. It's been months since she had pizza. All the Staten island crew been eating is canned foods and dry foods since the world ended. It was all that lasted.

"You look like you haven't seen a pizza before"

Paige responds with a joke that her ex told her about guys who take girls out on cheap dates.

"Is this the part where you tell me I can pick out anything on the dollar menu?"

Old man Tyrone can't help but laugh.

"You're a funny one. Something you learned from Frank I'm assuming."

Just then she got a feeling in her gut. *Did I just do something my Caps would have done?* She thought to herself while trying to eat.

Paige tried to push thoughts of her ex out of her mind. *No, No, No, snap out of it. Life or death here Paige. He's gone now.*

"No. just something I picked up from people back home."

Tyrone takes a sip of whine and nods.

"Ah, I see. Your ex then. My men tried to bring in the man who trained him for some questioning. But he didn't comply with us."

She couldn't believe he brought him up in conversation. How much these men know about the Staten Island crew.

"I have some intel but not much. Frank really isn't the brightest man. Too much of a pot head. He's good at convincing people to do things when high, guess you see that now"

Her eyes begin to tear up. The old man sees what he said hurt her. He takes out his handkerchief and sits next to her, offering it to wipe away the tears.

"Sorry. My old age gets me to say things bluntly sometimes. Why don't you and your mother get some rest. I have rooms prepared for you two."

Looking up into Tyrone's eyes she asks if her mother is ok.

"Yes, my dear. I have two guards waiting for you outside the doors. They will take you to your apartment. In there are two nurses with your mother. Your apartment is also next to Frank's."

Paige's smiles went straight when she heard that last line. Seeing this Tyrone tries to fix the situation.

"But I can have him moved till you're ready to be friends again."

Paige thanks him and walks towards the doors. But stops when the old man grabs her arm.

"I do need you to write down everything you know about the base. Food, ammunition, fuel, how man exits and entrances there is. And whatever you know about your former company's troops are like. I'll send my men to collect it in the morning."

The next morning Paige handed in most of what she remembered about the Staten Island base. The ten pages she handed in gave good amount of details of supplies. How much food and water were used daily, and how much would last through the next month. Even gave as close of an estimate on how much would last for the next 18 months with the consummation of supplies.

After two days of polite interrogation by Tyrone, Paige was shown around. Tyron let her have a radio to keep in contact with her mother if she ever felt the need to talk to her.

Not given any jobs but she stayed close to Tyron, taking in everything he said and did. She was impressed by the scale of his operations. Whole streets were dedicated to vehicles. One street section for trucks, another for SUVs. Fuel storage was placed in different areas so not one attack could take out their supply. Same went for food and water. To just drive around northern Brooklyn took three and a half days.

The drive was relaxing in the limo. No one dared showed any disrespect while she was with him. Everyone took off their hats when Tyron was near.

On the fourth day, Paige was given a job. She was to start recording and monitoring all supply routes coming in and out of Manhattan. She was excited to get back to work. To have the feeling of belonging again. Memories of the work she did back on Staten Island came to mind. Paige couldn't help but ask what was going to happen with the people she knew.

"What's going on with My peop. . . Staten Island?" Paige asks correcting herself.

"I'd rather not talk about that with you my dear. You shouldn't bother yourself with them any longer."

Paige turns her head and looks back out the limo window. She could see her reflection and Tyron's. He didn't show any signs of regret in his decision appointing her to her new job.

"I had some friends there. They always kept pushing me to leave my ex and hook me up with someone new. Will they be spared? Do you know who they are?"

Tyron places his hand on her knee in an attempt to show some trust. Then reply's,

“Honey of course they will be. Frank told me where they are located. Though I must ask, you sure they’re your friends? Though I am grateful they brought you to our side through their un-intentional actions, they did however try to hook you up with friends of theirs no? They don’t seem to have regards to your happiness but to improve their inner circle of friends.”

Paige couldn’t believe what she was hearing. Either he was trying to make excuses to not help them or convince her that they weren’t worth saving.

Tyron then took his hand off her and placed it back on the handle of his cane. Paige went back to looking out the window, opening it slightly. The air around Brooklyn smelled different. Might have been from the construction around her or the small number of vehicles moving around the areas they’ve been. But it was starting to smell like the city she knew a little over a year ago. The feeling of normalcy started to come back. Something she dreamed of with Caps.

That last thought made what Tyron said about her friends sink. Her mind started to race again. She looked in her bag for her flask. It was gone. A shot glass was then put in front of her by Tyron. “A little birdy told me that you like Jack Daniels” He said as he poured the drink.

The limo stopped in front of the Manhattan Bridge. A small building was built on the side. It looked like a small house.

Again, impressed at the work that was done Paige asked, “How did you build this?”

“Saved some construction workers when the world ended. These were some high-end sheds that I had them convert to a house. This will be your office. You are to check in tomorrow. You’ll be sleeping here for two days out of the week for now. I want to see what else you can do besides cataloging inventory. I’ll have guards posted with you at all times. Work starts tomorrow.”

The following morning Paige was brought to her new job with her new team and a few bodyguards. With some excitement she went to work cataloging and checking each truck that came across from Manhattan.

Once and a while some of the dead would show up in groups. Each time the guards would take them out using spears made from iron construction bars.

Two days passed and her shift then went to the next person. Another women. She was tall and heavy looking. Paige tried to introduce herself.

"Hey I'm Paige. Guess you'll be taking over from here huh?"

The women ignored her and just dug herself into the paperwork from the previous days. An awkward moment passed while Paige stood there, waiting for some orders from the women. Finally, she looked up, looked right into Paige's blue eyes and replied, "Why you still here?"

With that said, Paige takes her leave back to the apartment, only for the women to run out and hand her an envelope that said "materials". The heavy-set women seemed annoyed. When Paige opened up the envelope it was a shorter version of the cataloged materials that she worked so hard to get in order. Then a sticky note on the bottom. It read "You suck at this landfill. Should have stayed on your island". Paige runs back inside and shouts at the woman.

"What the fuck is your problem!?"

The heavy women steps forward towards her, she towers over Paige. Looming up and trying not to show fear she demands an answer.

"Well?! What is it?"

The heavy-set women gets down to eye level with her. A clear sign that she doesn't respect Paige. She gives a short reply.

"I don't like you. Your name here is landfill for now on. Just like your island, you fill every hole you have with the biggest pieces of shit there is."

Paige knew she was talking about Frank. But not the reason as to why. Then the heavy women gave a demand.

"You are not to talk to me, don't even look in my direction. You are only alive because of the big man. Now get lost."

Paige walked back towards the door and shut it quickly. Noticing the guards looking at her, Paige hid her tears as best she could as she got in her armored car.

A ride which should have taken a few minutes, took over forty minutes to get back home. One of the buildings on route had an outbreak. Paige tried to get answers from her bodyguards, but they all told her to stay in the armored car with them and wait for the Crypt gang to clear out the building. Newly infected could be seen trying to run out of the building. Memories of the first few days of the apocalypse ran through Paige's mind. How these fast moving infected were far more terrifying then the dead. She couldn't help but stare at the carnage. Anyone who was inside was shot if they tried to leave.

Seeing this wasn't something too new to her. Caps told her stories about what he and Jacob did. How even children had to be executed if they had been infected. She remembered how one night he came back home three days early. He just sat on the floor in the door, crying as he did so. She remembered how it took him days to finally say what he did, what he had to do at the kindergarten school by his home. She remembered every detail about what he went through. It was stuff straight from a mother's nightmare. How he couldn't help any of them. She then remembered how her hand hurt after she slapped Jacob for making her boyfriend do all he did. She remembered how she demanded answers as well.

"How could you make him do that!? He wanted to be a teacher you MORON!" Jacob never responded. Just put his head down and walked away. It was two weeks before her Caps went back out. She forgave him for what he had to do. Because he was honest with her. He never hid how he was feeling.

Her memory then made her question what she was seeing. The Crypts didn't seem to care who it was they were shooting. None of the Crypts even checked people for wounds. They just kept shooting on sight. Twice they tried to move in, twice they were pushed back.

Then it happened. Something she hasn't seen since she was a child when watching the news on 9/11. People were jumping out of the windows. The building was now on fire as well. It was then that they were given the go to move through.

Once back home Paige looked to one of the guards and asked who she hands her paperwork to.

"The boss is in the Lower lobby. Head there and he will brief you on what to do next."

Paige asks, "You're not coming?"

"We'll be waiting out here till we get further orders. Other guards here know who you are. If you try to leave, you'll will be caught."

As Paige opened the door, she sees a truck pulling into the garage at a high speed. When it came to a sudden stop two men pulled out a woman. Paige immediately knew who it was. It was Pauline.

Paige ran inside and past the guards in front of Tyrone's office. Slamming her paperwork on his table.

"I want to speak with her!" She shouts.

Tyrone leans back in his chair and smokes weed from his pipe. The room is silent. A click can be heard from the two guards in his office. It was the sound of their safety being taken off their submachine guns.

"She's being prepared to be sent back. Prisoner exchange. None of your concern my dear."

Paige relaxed her body when realizing how she looked. She heard another click when she stepped back.

"Is she alright?" She asked with a emotional tone.

Tyrone gets up and puts his pipe down. He walks over to her and holds her by the shoulders and replies.

"Of course, honey. She'll be going home. We want her to tell your homies back home to surrender."

Paige looks around the room and sees how she just mad an ass out of herself.

"Go see your mum. I'll send for you later"

Chapter 12

Middle of the night

Later that night Paige went down to the area that Pauline was being held. Seeing guards in front of a door in the basement she had two thoughts.

She must be in there.

Wait. . . What am I doing?

She paced back and forth by the broken elevators, wondering what to do next. Ideas came and went. Not a fighter and not very good at confrontations left her with severe limits. Stopping in front of her reflection on the elevator doors and banging her head lightly she kept thinking. It was then that it hit her. Her position in her new group.

Walking like she owned the place; Paige walked straight up to the guards and made a demand.

"I'm here to see the prisoner."

Both guards just looked at her and laughed. Not amused by this Paige snapped another demand.

"I need to know what she knows to help us! Now either you two shits let me in to question the prisoner or I'm telling the big man how you wouldn't let an investigator go through. Then I'll be cutting your rations. Got it!"

Both guards went silent. Seconds later one of the guards grabbed his keys and opened the door. As Paige stepped through and heard the door behind her close she internally screamed, *I can't believe that worked!*

Walking down the hall she sees a hand handcuffed to a heater. A plate with crumbs is next to her.

Paige whispers. "Pauline. That you? Are you ok?"

Pauline turns around and sees Paige. Her blue eyes reflecting the light.

"Oh my God! Paige you got to get me outta here fast. Before he comes back!"

Paige just stood there. She saw what Pauline was wearing. Just a sweatshirt and two different color knee high socks. One cheek was red. Like she was hit.

"Paige! What are you doing? Get over here and help. Where's the others?"

Lowering her head Paige thinks of what to say.

"What are you doing!" Pauline shouts.

"They're not coming."

"What?"

Taking a nearby crate, Paige sits near her. "I just wanted to make sure you were ok. Johnny was about to tell me what happened when he found out. . ."

Paige pauses and turns red as embarrassment sets in. Stuttering when she tries to get the words out. But she doesn't know what she's saying. Her speech is incoherent.

"What are you saying!? Just get me out before he comes back."

Paige responds crying. "I can't!" I'm with them now"

Pauline's eyes squinted as she tried to process what she heard. Anger is vividly seen on her face as she listens to what Paige tries to explain what she did.

"He didn't appreciate me! I did everything for him in the beginning. He never! Ever! Even thanked me for it. I slept with someone else. He listens to me. He smokes with me."

Sitting on the cold floor Pauline just stares as she realizes she's not getting out. Listening to her sobbing just made her angry. But she listened knowing that any outburst can take away any chance of her getting free.

"Things got physical. He pushed me. You're a victim of domestic violence, right? You understand why I did this right?"

Pauline recoils back as Paige tries to reach for her hand. Her facial expression showing disgust over what she just heard. With no way out she argues back.

"Our situations are not at all the same! You cheated and now want to recruit people to your side. I doubt he hit you. I hooked him up with people waaaay before you two met. He never hurt anyone that he dated."

Paige pulls back her hand and steps back. Tripping on a lose pipe as she does so. Now looking up at Pauline, it now looks as if she's being talked down to. Making her now feeling powerless in this conversation. Pauline's words now hit her hard.

"Are you really that dumb? Look around! Look where I am. Things were getting better for everyone! You fucked that all up."

Paige turns around, gets up, and starts walking away. She walks faster as Pauline shouts at her.

"Traitor! All you care about is yourself! You're going to jump from relationship to relationship. Johnny might be a bit nuts at times but at least he's loyal and works things out. Good luck finding Mr. Perfect among these users and manipulators! CUNT!"

Pausing at the door Paige contemplates what to say. But nothing right comes to mind. She doesn't want to listen but can't stop herself from wanting to hear what they have to say.

"You were manipulated by people who wanted you took hook up with their people, their crew."

Paige turns around, hearing the tone in her voice change. She listened knowing Pauline was right.

"The fake grass they showed you on the other side might look greener, but when it breaks apart you won't be able to fix it. It doesn't grow like the real thing. Because it was fake. You had real grass with him, with us."

Before shutting the door behind her, Paige sees Pauline's face one last time. Light from the open door slowly diminishes as she slowly shuts it.

Hiding her tears from the guards at the door, Paige went back to her room and got ready for the next day.

Chapter 13

A week later after he left

Even with ear plugs and a bag over her head, Pauline could still hear the wind howl. The Brooklyn Knights stood behind her with rifles at her back, pushing her forward every time she slowed down. She couldn't see what was in front of her, which made each step a carful one.

This past week had been hell. Every night Pauline was visited by Michael. She had the bruises in between her legs to prove it. Her wrists itched due to the scabs left by the hand cuffs. Each breath was hard to take in. The duct tape around her mouth made breathing through her noise her only option. Made harder due to the bag. She walked with an empty stomach. Only meals she was given was bread and water, and that was two days ago.

She knew it was morning out when sunlight hit her. She couldn't see much through the bag but as the sun rose, and touched her, she could make out some silhouettes of stuff nearby. Cars, roadblocks, and bodies littered the area around her. She was able to make out some chairs close by with a small table.

One of the Brooklyn Knights pulled her bag off. She was able to measure up the two men by her own height. They must have been over 6 feet tall. She was 5'10 and they were at least a head taller by her estimate. Pushing her to the floor one of the two shouts "Sit there and keep your fucking mouth shut!"

Not long after leaning against a tire she could see a car driving up to them. It stopped some distance away. Out stepped four men in military camouflage. She knew this had to be a prisoner exchange. Looking around her Pauline could see some Brooklyn Knights were hiding nearby. She could see their feet under the cars. But that wasn't what terrified her. She noticed the back of a truck. It said *¡No abrir! Gente muerta adentro!*. It was written in red, so she knew it was bad. She wanted to warn her friends but couldn't get the duct tape off her mouth.

Looking back at her friends she noticed something. They were wearing masks. Two of them were skulls, the others were clowns.

One of the two Brooklyn Knights held out his hand and demanded her friends to stop. Then asked where their man was. One of the clowns went to the trunk of the car and pulled out their captive. Pauline can see he was hurt. The bag on his head was white, with blood stains on one side. One of the Skulls then walked up to the chairs and sat down. One of the two Brooklyn Knights then walked up the other chair and sat. Pauline listened in as best she could.

"So, you wanna show me yours and I'll show you mine? Mine is sitting right there."

The Brooklyn Knight smiled and pointed with his thumb behind him. Confidence shown on his face.

"She's a looker, isn't she? Those freckles and red hair. Oh, I wish I got to have some fun with her."

The soldier wearing the skull mask didn't say anything. Didn't even move.

"So, you're Darin Joseph. You dumb asses always wear name tags. You act like there's still order in this world. Like we didn't know you were going to get information from our boys in any way possible."

The Brooklyn Knight leans in closer. Smiling, he tries his best to look him in the eye. He whispers "You're just as bad as us"

Again, there was no reply. Darin lifts his hand and waves for one of the other soldiers to bring over their captive.

The Brooklyn Knight waves as well. The second knight picks Pauline up and brings her over by the table, pointing a gun at her head.

"Now, take off the bag. I wanna see if that's really my boy."

Soldier clown takes off the blood gang member's bag. The Brooklyn Knight is shocked at what he sees. His ear is chopped off, his face has slash marks on it. Eyes are blood red. Clearly sleep deprived.

"DA FUCK IS THIS SHIT!" He screams.

He flips over his chair and points his gun at Darin. Again, there's no reaction. Realizing that breaking the peace would mean breaking orders, he lowers his pistol.

"Orders. . . they fucking suck, am I right?"

Again, there's no answer. Just a blank stare with a head tilt.

"Whatever. Ok take your whore. My boy back home loosened her up for ya."

Turning around he begins to walk away with his fellow blood. Then he hears Darin say something

♪ Their ain't no strings on me ♪

The Brooklyn Knight turns back around to see Darin pointing a flair gun straight up in the air. Slowly he takes a few steps closer while asking "The fuck you say homie?"

♪ So, I have fun ♪

The Brooklyn Knight sees what's going on. He starts to step back. Holding his pistol pointed at Darin.

♪ I'm not tied up to anyone, you've got string ♪

Darin fires his flair gun. The Brooklyn Knight backs and shouts, "You're breaking the fucking truce! We had a fucking deal!"

♪ But you can see, ♪

♪ There are no strings on me ♪

With that last verse the men Pauline saw jump up from behind their cars and tackle the Brooklyn Knights.

"What the fuck you doing!" He screams as he's hand cuffed. Darin shoots the second Brooklyn Knight in the head.

"You mother fuckers! You agreed to a truce! You agreed!"

Darin squats down in front of him as the rest help Pauline back up. Pulling out his pistol he shoots old blood captive in the head.

"You said earlier that I was just as bad as you. Nooooo."

The knight realizing he's been tricked asks "Who the fuck you think you are?!"

Pulling off his mask he say's "I'm far, far worse!"

Pauline watches as he pulls off his mask and reviles that it's really Caps.

"You're coming with me. I need someone new to play with."

Caps dragged the Knight by his legs to the back of the truck with red letters. Tying the man's handcuffs to the car handle just opposite of the truck with red letters on it. Pulling out a small amount of explosive, Caps sets it on the locks of the truck doors.

"What are you doing!? Are you crazy!?" The man screams.

Pausing, only for a moment. He turns around quickly and again squats down to eye level with the Knight.

"I'm having a pretty bad week. Well . . . not as bad as you're about to have. I want information." Caps says as he points his remote explosive charge in the man's face.

"See you guys are planning something. I know this because me and my cousins here have been taking out your outposts. And killing your men one by one all week . . . well, sort of."

Caps gets up and bangs on the truck. Snarling and growling can be heard loudly. The Knight's eyes widen as he realizes what awaits him on the other side.

"You kidnapped some of us. There will be no peace. I don't care about what the higher ups say. You hurt people I care about. Now you gonna tell me where she is?

The knight points with his hands, "She's right there man!"

Not amused by this, Caps takes his pistol out and pistol whips the knight in the mouth. Breaking his front teeth. Caps asks again.

"Where is my girl?! I want to know where you took Paige!"

The Knight pisses himself. And claims he doesn't know. About to hit the man again Pauline suddenly shouts, "I do. I know"

Caps lowers his gun and picks the man up. His cousins take off their masks and put the Knight in the trunk of their car.

Driving off the bridge Caps takes Pauline to their hideout. The turns she made along her route. Caps using a map did the best he could to draw up where she was being held. She tells him about the conversation she had with Paige. Soon they came to his hide out. A comic bookstore called Comic Book Jones.

One of Caps cousins named Nadine checks Pauline's wounds. Her toe is broken, her wrists are cut and bloody, not just from the handcuffs. It looked like a suicide attempt; then she examined the bruises on her inner thighs. Nadine goes to the back room and gets out a rape kit. Caps and the rest of the cousins close the shades and give them privacy. As the ladies talk the men try not to listen as Pauline starts to cry loudly.

Some time passed and Nadine briefed them on her condition. She then pleaded with her cousin.

"You have to take her back to base. She needs more help than what we, well I, can do here."

Caps sat down and pulled out his pistol. He stared at it. Emptying out the clip, he tried to keep himself busy in thought. Nadine stops him and holds his hands and pleads with him.

"You have to. This isn't . . . isn't something that you can talk to her about just yet. You can't be head strong, you can't fight for her right now, she needs time to heal. Not just physically but emotionally. Please tell Darin to take her back."

Pauline pulls back the curtains and ask's "What's this about Darin?" She said as she tried to walk straight. Nadine was the first to catch her as she stumbled. Caps then stood up and asked his cousins Anthony and Pete to get Darin and his men from their cells.

"Caps, why are they locked up?" Pauline asks.

"I kind of had no choice. We saw that the Brooklyn Knights had men in reserve, and we had to act."

Darin, Mac and Someone they called the new guy were escorted in by the cousins.

"Darin, we have an issue. . . Oh shit!"

Not holding back Darin throws a punch right into Caps left cheek. Rolling with the punch Caps was able to keep his footing. His cousins broke up the fight before it went any further.

Pauline was confused and couldn't help but ask "Uh guys, what's going on?"

"It's ok. I deserved it."

Darin still angry broke out from the cousin's grip, punching Caps once again. Falling back on his ass and getting up quickly, he signals that's its ok before telling Pauline,

"That one too. Ok so I might have had Darin locked up for a bit. He was going to just let the captive be exchanged and was going to be set up in the ambush. So, in a sense I saved not only your life, but his as well."

Darin then tries to kick Caps in the balls.

"Ok woaaaah, not the gems ok. You done?"

Pauline yells for Darin to stop. Then confirms Caps story.

"What he said is true. They had people already on the bridge. They were waiting in ambush."

Sarcastically Caps looks to Darin and says "You're welcome"

Not amused Darin turns to Pauline and asks, "Are you alright?"

"I'm angry!" She says doing her best to stand up.

"I wanna kill them. We have to go back out there." She says shaking."

Nadine again catches her as she falls. Pulling Darin aside, Caps asks him to take her and his cousins back home. He hands Darin the keys to a car parked outside.

"Where you going then?"

Caps pulls out the map and draws a circle around an area he thinks Paige is. Darin realizing that Caps isn't coming back with him offers to help, but Caps refused.

"Damn it Johnny. If you're not going to come back with us, then at least let me give you a parting gift. You take any maps with you from those assholes?"

They go to the trunk of the car and pull out their new captive and search his pockets. There's a map with some markings but most where erased. The Knight laughs as he thinks to himself that they will never be able to find what they're looking for. Caps takes out brass knuckles, but just as he was about to hit him, Darin stops him.

"What? We can get answers from him this way, easy."

Shaking his head Darin replies "Just watch. This is how you get what you want.

Pulling out a pencil Darin places the map on the hood of the car. Then takes a piece of thin white paper and places it on top of the map. He begins to scribble on it. The indents from previous markings showed up on the white sheet. One of the markings says HQ. Seeing this the Knight suddenly stopped laughing. Darin waved the map in front of him and then handed it to Caps.

"This is why you never made squad leader. Use your brain. It's your best weapon."

Moments later when everyone packed up the two cars with their supplies and a few comic books, Darin asked one last time if he would like to come back.

"I got to find her."

Darin leans to his car window. "No, you don't. We still don't know what her state of mind is."

"She was manipulated by that asshole and some friends"

"Caps we don't know that for sure. For all we know she could have been working with him all along. Just come back with us. Commander Caladonato will be needing every man we have to defend our island."

Caps just closes his eyes and shakes his head.

Darin tries one last time to convince his friend to come home. "Look Johnny, you might have gone off the rails this past week. But you did a hell of a lot of good too. You destroyed seven outposts these assholes made in just seven days. You and your cousins won't be reprimanded. I'll make sure of that."

"I'm sorry but I got to do this. I need to know if she's ok. I was too busy for her before. I have to do this."

His cousin Pete sticks his head out of the car window and ask's, "If you don't make it back can I have your Xbox?"

"No. and You're a dick" Caps reply laughing.

Pauline pulls caps to the side and tells him what she and Paige talked about.

"She's not the same. She's been doing this to you for a while. She was talking to guys who wanted to fuck her while you were together. They got her to change sides while you were working on a making a better life. She's confused. I know you want her back, but she's too far manipulated."

Caps didn't respond. Just gave a head nod and thanked her for telling him what she knew.

Knocking on the roof of the car Caps wished them good luck getting back to base. He then sat in his own car and leaned his head back, closing his eyes for a moment to think of his next move, when suddenly his back-car doors open. Two of his cousins jump in.

"You really think we going to let you go alone?" Pete says.

"You guys don't need to come"

Responding sarcastically Chris replies "I know but we drew straws and we lost"

Pete joking punches him in the arm. Caps just smiles and starts driving. Both cars leave in separate directions.

Leaning forward in between the two front seats Chris asks, "So what's the plan?"

Caps didn't respond. All week he was able to wing it when it came to tactics. But now he's at a loss. Only one idea came to mind. It was how to get there.

"Your dad had a boat at the docks, right? We can't go by land. So maybe we can go by sea."

Chapter 14

Pirate Raider looking for his booty

About an hour into the voyage, Chris was still singing pirate songs. As annoying as it was, it helped curb the sea sickness Pete was suffering from. Twice he threw up, one of those times was on Capp's boots.

Chris shouts out "Land hooo!" and points to Governors Island. Caps wanted to argue that this was far off where they needed to be but felt sick from the waves and Chris's driving.

Docking, Chris jumps out and ties the boat to the Railing. Pete stumbles out of the boat, holding his stomach as he does so. Caps takes out some binoculars and looks around at the buildings. As he checks each window for movement Chris tries to joke with everyone.

"I name this land in the name of the Louers! We are a proud people and-"

Chris's speech is cut short by loud growling in the distance. Caps looks in the direction of the noise. The container redemption center had its door open. Hordes of dead were now coming out and heading straight for them. They were stopped by the gated fence in front of the pier. But it wouldn't hold for long. Bodies were now pushing each other forwards into the gate.

Quickly Chris and Pete Jump back in the boat while Caps unties it from the railing. The amount of dead pushing against the gate with no locks bent the thin metal that kept it closed. Now they were coming in closer, but the trio were too far out to be eaten alive. Still the dead tried to reach them. The dead didn't care what got in their way. Many pushed each other off the pier by accident. Many just kept walking in the direction of the boat, falling off the pier and submerging themselves in the water. Some floated for a bit but all were taken under. More were now coming from the rest of the island.

Chris turns back to his cousins. Sarcastically he remarks, "Well I guess I'm conquered huh?"

Just as he said that, rain started to fall. All three move fast to put up the boat roof. Chris gets back behind the wheel and starts driving again. Caps takes one final look at the island. He can see on the roof there were words written in white paint. It read "Help Us!"

Twenty minutes passed. Caps kept looking for a suitable place to land. He kept looking towards Brooklyn Heights but all he saw was men with guns and spears.

Barricades on almost every street he could see. Chris starts driving the boat to the docks near a building with the sign that read “Party Rentals” on it. When asked why he was moving Chris replied “We can hide behind the containers”

“Can we just get off the fucking water already?” Pete said loudly.

Docking the boat, Caps grabs some crates and elevates himself above the steal container. Looking around he sees no Brooklyn Knights and very few dead.

A few minutes passed as they waited for Pete to recuperate from sea sickness. A truck was no pulling into the yard and headed straight for them. All three jumped back into the boat, putting a tarp over them to give some sort of hiding space. Then they listened.

The Knight’s opened up the containers and began unloading and then loading their trucks. One of the men shouted that they would be back later.

When the truck was far enough away the trio investigated. The container had Solar panels in it.

“They must get by, by raiding these docks.” Pete said as he knocked one hand on the container.

One of the ships nearby had a tall mast. Climbing to the top, Caps looking through his binoculars could see all the way to Brooklyn Bridge Park. Though most of his view was blocked by a transportation warehouse. A makeshift wall was built using shipping containers. From what he could see it stretched down Atlantic Ave. A wide double gate was on Columbus Street. Guards were dotted along the wall. Many armed just with spears. There were no walls in between them so all could see each other. Making it impossible to take a few out and go around.

Rain began to fall harder. Many of the guards stayed under their canopies. Still able to see each other. But then he sees it. The guards at the gate didn't bother to check the park behind them.

As the rain fell it hit the containers around them. The noise wasn't deafening but enough that it could give them some cover. Caps came up with a plan. He turned to his two cousins and tried to explain as best he could his idea.

"Back in World War Two, Germany tricked France into looking in another direction for a big attack. Then they punched through the opposite side of the Maginot Line."

"You're giving us a history lesson because?"

"We don't need to take out all the guards. Just find some way to make them think that they are being hit from somewhere else."

For a good twenty minutes the trio discussed what to do. Pete came up with the plan in the end since he's from Brooklyn and knew how to get around better in the city than both Chris and Caps. Using some explosives, Pete set up a timed bomb to go off within ten minutes at a coffee shop on the corner of Atlantic and Hicks street.

Chris and Caps watch the guards for their reactions. Pete counted down on his watch in excitement for the oncoming explosion.

"3, 2, 1 boom" He whispered.

There was no boom. Not even a fizzle came out of the coffee shop.

"Did you fuck up setting the explosives?" Chris whispered in an agitated tone.

Suddenly the ground shook with a defining boom as the room and windows of the coffee shop blew outwards. All guards turned their attention towards the explosion. The ones they needed to pass were looking through their own binoculars to see the carnage.

Quickly the trio went around the edge of the crates and into the park behind them. Their muddy footsteps washed away by the rain that was now coming down harder. The sound of thunder dwarfed the explosion that they made just moments ago and the wind that followed it knocked over one of the guards who was trying to get under some cover. As he stood up, he sees three men run up to him. One holds him from behind, another holds his mouth shut, the last cuts his throat and stabs him in the head. Blood shoots out, but it too is washed away by the rain. The trio then tosses his lifeless body into the water and run to get some cover in a nearby food court. The lights where on which meant that someone might be inside. They climbed through the window in case there was a bell on the door.

As they contemplated their next move, Chris grabs some rags to dry his face and hands some to his cousins. Just as he was about to speak, they hear some voices in the room next to him. They all crouch down and move closer to hear anything that might help them.

"Fuck you guys! Straight!" one-man shouts as he throws his cards on the table.

“Well fag I got a flush. So, I’ll be taking this” Another man says as he grabs the chips off the table.

Pete uses a mirror to see how many people are in the room. Once getting a good enough view he turns and uses sign language, signaling that 4 were in the room, 3 were sitting around a table.

“Both of you are losers.” A woman shouts from the torn-up couch in the room.

“Bitch you just mad that you lost early on”

“No limp dick, I just didn’t want to play.”

“Uh huh”

“Fuck y’all, I’m going to go pee.” She struggles to get up, then struggles picking up a bucket near the door.

Pete’s eyes widen when he sees why. She’s pregnant. He signs with his hands to move away. Quickly they scurry into the kitchen. As she walks to struggles to light a cigarette. Oblivious to her surroundings, she walks past them, not even noticing Chris’s foot sticking out of the doorway. Her cigarette lights up when she comes to the door. Pulling down her pants she squats down and uses the bucket as a toilet. Her other hand holding an iPod to play music on her big headphones.

Chris takes out his knife and slowly approaches her. In his head he said a prayer for the unborn child he had to kill by accident. Inching closer to almost arm's length Caps grabs his shoulder and shakes his head no. Pulling his cousin aside, Caps then approaches her with a rolling pin in one hand.

The women get's up and opens the door in front of her to toss the buckets contents outside. The bells on the door rang as she did so. Turning around she sees Caps for a second before being knocked out cold. Her cigarette still lit in her mouth.

All three turn around and listen. Pete signals to follow him. Chris takes the cigarette out of the women's mouth and starts smoking. As they get close to the room, they can hear the men inside talking.

Then one shouts "Hey Claire! You alright? You get stuck in the bucket again?"

"Prego bitch! He talking to you"

"She's probably outside smoking again. Shaqquan go check on that ho since you out of chips"

"Nigga I got chips; you check"

“First of all, you half white, so you can’t be saying our fucking word! Got it!? Second you got three mother fucking chips. Third do it before I put my foot in your ass.”

“Man. . . fuck y’all”

As the man gets up Pete signals once again for them to back up into the kitchen. This time Chris pays attention to his feet. Making sure they’re not exposed. The Brooklyn Knight walks through the door and passed the kitchen, rolling a blunt as he does so. Once passed the kitchen door he looks up with a full rolled blunt and sees Claire on the floor, bleeding from the head unconscious.

“Oh Shiiit” He says stepping back.

He quickly turns around and sees Caps. He tries to shout but his throat is cut. All he could do now is hold his neck and hope to stop the bleeding. Chris tries to grab the man as he fell, but his body falls down and hits the table next to him. Knocking over a plate and some cups.

“Prego you fall down again?!” one of the men from inside the rooms shouts.

With no time to hide the body the trio got ready to fight. The odds were now 3 to 2 in their favor.

Not hearing a response, the Brooklyn Knights take out their pistols. As one approaches the door, he tries one last time to communicate with his friends.

"Clair, Shaqquan! You guys alright?"

With no response he turns his head and tells the other Knight to get on the radio and call for back up. He steps out the door with pistol raised. As he quickly passes the kitchen Pete and Chris simultaneously try to stop him. He lunges his knife. Attempting to stab the man in his hands to stop him from firing a shot, by accident he stabs into the Knight's fingers. The knife now stuck behind the trigger. Pete holds his mouth as Chris using a butcher's knife stabs the man repeatedly before stabbing him in the head.

Caps runs into the room with his rifle in hand and sees the knight trying to get the radio to work.

"Hands! Let me see your hands!" Caps shouts.

The Knight puts both his hands up.

"I surrender. Don't shoot!"

Caps rushes towards him but the knight starts shooting into the air. Hoping someone would hear the shots. But the rain and thunder kept the noise from reaching his comrades. Caps knocks the man out cold before cutting his throat and stabbing him in the head.

Pete checks out the radio. Flicking the power button on and off he looks under the table. He shows Caps the plug.

“Dumb asses forgot to plug this in”

Chris walks in and points behind him.

“Guys! She’s awake”

All three run back to the pregnant women. She was trying to push open the door when Pete and Caps grabbed her by her legs, pulling her back in.

Chris runs to the janitor’s closet and looks for anything to tie her down with. Finding duct tape he runs back only to see Chris being bitten on the hand. He screams in pain and punches her right in the eye with his other hand. He women falls to the floor, and once again she’s unconscious.

‘Holy shit! Is she. . . are you!?”

“Relax. She’s alive. Bitch just was just trying to get away is all”

Half an hour later the women wake’s up. Duct tape all over her body. She’s taped to a chair. The trio staring at her. Caps is the first to speak.

“I going to remove the duct tape off your mouth. If you scream it’s going back on. You understand?”

She responds by nodding. Quickly removing the tape, he then starts to ask questions.

“There was a woman. She was kidnapped last week. I need to know where she is. You hear anything?”

The women shakers her head no. Then asks, “You got a cigarette?”

Chris responds for them. Stepping forward as he does so.

“You’re a real dumb cunt you know that?”

The women spit out a wad of flehm and blood at his feet. She replies, “Yeah well at least I’m not some little dick Irish boy who knocks out 16-year-old pregnant girls for fun”

Chris was about to answer back when Caps shouts “Enough!”

“Look. I could have let my cousin kill you back there. But I didn’t let him. I just want to know where my girlfriend is. I give you my word that I'll let you live and leave a note or radio in that you're tied up here when I get her out. Just tell me where she might be."

The women mumbled something and begins to pass out. Caps moves in closer to listen. As he tries to hear what she has to say, she then shouts demanding for one thing.

"I want my fucking cigarettes!"

Pete quickly puts back on the duct tape. All three then take a few steps back and huddle together.

"What you guys thinking?" Chris asks.

"I won't torture a pregnant woman. No matter how bitchy she is.

Pete then walks back up to her, rips off the tape, puts a cigarette in her mouth and lights it. His cousins look on. Not knowing how to respond. Pete lifts up her sleeve on her short sleeve shirt. Pointing he tells his cousins, "She's a junkie. Or at least was. She wants a cigarette to keep the edge off."

The women's facial expression was now in bliss as she huffed her smokes. Patiently they waited till she finished. When she got down to the filter, she spit it on the floor.

"Go another?" She asks with a smile.

With disgust, Pete pulls another one out of her pack. But this time he smokes it himself. Caps then grabs her attention by spinning her around towards him.

"Tell me what you know, and I'll let you have one."

"Alright sugar."

Caps pulls over a chair to listen at her eye level.

"Word is your girl left you for some trash talker."

"So, I've heard. What else?"

"She's now working for us. But most likely she's off today since my boo is working her shift."

After saying that she stops talking. Caps waits, thinking she's trying to remember. But a minute passes before she says "That's it"

"What you mean?"

"Mother fucker what you think I mean? I mean that's all I know. What? You thought I would know where your cracka ass girlfriend is? Bitch she cheated on you for some shit head who uses women. Get over it and go home."

Sitting back in his chair, he looks to his cousins. But they shook their heads, not knowing what to do. That's when she makes a suggestion.

"Only place I could possibly think of is the club."

"The club?

"Yeah white boy! The mother fucking club! I know you boys are white as bread, but you know what dancing is. It's where everyone goes to unwind. Literally down the block."

Pete looks out the window and sees some purple light coming from a building on bridge park dr. He then turns the women towards him, with his hand he made it seem like he was going to put the cigarette in her mouth but drops it to the floor. Then empties out the pack onto her lap.

Caps gets a new strip of duct tape. Right as he's putting on the new strip, Claire moves and dodges to avoid being gagged.

"Wait! I can help you get in!"

Pausing. He listens to what she has to say. He notices her eyes starting to tear up.

"You can't get in shooting up the place. Sneaking maybe but there's too many. You also dress too much like white preppy boys. . . Well except you Rambo."

"Great so where's the closest ghetto shop." Chris says with sarcasm.

Pete points with his index finger at the bodies around them. "Right here"

Moments later, after the trio dressed. Clair looked at Chris and commented on the trios looks.

"White boy you and your freckles will have a tough time blending in. But you two, y'all can pass for Hispanic . . . I guess."

Chris looks at his cousins and waits for them to come to his defense. But they agree with Clair

Caps curious asks "Ok so why help us."

"I'm not helping them. I'm helping you."

"What?"

Clair looks out the window in the direction of the light. She takes a deep breath in to try and hold back her tears before responding.

"Your girl must be important. From what I heard two of your buddies were captured. One was tortured. The other was given a job because she was skilled. But from what I hear she hasn’t been much help. Only matter of time before he. . . he!”

Claire starts sobbing. She tries to wipe her tears away. Caps grabs a rag and does it for her. She bites her lip, trying to hold back more tears.

“There’s a man in there. Big guy, yellow teeth. His hair is receding but that don’t stop that ugly mother fucker from slicking it back. His name is Michael.”

She looks at her belly with teary eyes.

“The baby is his. . .I didn’t want it. She’s not going to want hers either.”

Chris and Pete’s jaws drop at what they just heard. Caps grips his pistol in anger. His eye didn’t blink, his breathing was still.

“I don’t know what you plan on doing. But when Tyrone finds no use for her, he’s sending her to him.”

Caps pulls out his knife. Claire is hit with fear and panic. She can’t speak, pissing herself, she can only make noises. He grabs her chair and cuts her out of her duct tape restraints. She looks at him confused.

Getting to eye level with her Caps tells her, “I want you to run. Go find a hiding place and don’t come out till this war is over.”

He then turns to his cousins and signals it's time to go. They grab the umbrellas by the doors and head out.

"If you see him in there. Kill him. . . Please kill him"

Caps nods and tells her to take care of herself.

Chapter 15

Little Shop of Horrors

As they approached the club, they can hear the beats from music playing inside. Its muffled from the soundproof doors.

“My pistol is riding up against my crotch. You sure we can’t just put it around out ankle’s? Chris asks.

“The way these guys talk sounds like they’re homophobes. Most likely they won’t check our junk. So just keep it there for now. Just wish I could bring my rifle.”

Smiling Pete and says “Just cause we’re Sicilian I don’t think they would think our junk is as long as your rifle. Saying we’re part black because of our southern heritage wouldn’t be enough.”

“You guys done? Ok let’s do this”

All three walk in wearing wet doorags, baggy pants, and shirts with money signs and rap lyrics on them. The bouncers at the door first look at each other and laugh when they see Chris. His freckles and light skin pop out more because of his dark outfit.

The bouncer on the right pats Chris down then tells him, “Alright whitey. You clean. Next!”

Pete and Caps get patted down. Both bouncers tell each other that the person they checked is clean. The darker bouncer stops Caps and asks in Spanish “Bet you loved to suck a dick in prison?”

Caps not knowing only two words in Spanish just laughs nervously and says “si” nodding along. Both guards laugh and open the doors for them.

Once the doors close behind them Pete asks Caps what they said to him.

“I have no idea. I can’t believe they bought it. They really thought I was like Puerto Rican or something.”

At the same time on the other side of the doors the guards were still laughing. The bald one said to the other guard “Caucasians. They crack me up.”

Back on the other side of the door the trio looks around at the club. It’s one main dance floor with a second and third level. Giant cages that mimic bird cages have dancers in them. Blondes, brunettes, red heads, black White, Asian, even a bald woman was in one. All are topless.

Pete trying to be heard but also trying to be quiet says to his cousins “Let’s try and blend in. Let's go to the bar and try and listen to. . . "

Caps gets Pete to look near the bar. He points to Chris who is dancing between two busty attractive black women. When they get closer to the bar they can hear Chris ask the bartender "Yo Bartender! Can you serve some milk for this Oreoooo!"

Leaning to Caps' ear Pete tells him "Well he's got the right idea"

Barely able to hear his cousin, Caps uses sign language to tell him to look up three floors above the door. Looking up both see a VIP section that oversees the entire club. Getting Pete's attention again he signs telling them to split up and see if they can find a way up there and meet back at the bar in 8 minutes.

Walking around and dancing at random times and places Caps walks into the storage room. A distillery is there. Brass containers and pipes are shining. He turns around to see the bar tender bringing in a few empty crates.

"Let me guess, looking for the bathroom?"

Caps shakes his head yes.

"Out this door and to the right. Then it's the first door on the right. Next to the exit sign."

Acting drunk to not raise and suspicion he acts as if he's losing his balance like a drunk person would. Once back on the dance floor he looks around. Looking back at the VIP section he sees someone smoking a cigar. Two women are next to him. One in a red dress, the other wearing black. But the one in black had a big white skull on it. The white glowed with the black lights around her.

Knowing Paige's style, he thought to himself. *That must be her!*

Asking the nearest person where the stairs were, they pointed over to where the bartender said the bathrooms where.

When he came near the stairs, he saw Frank senior going down carrying a big wooden box. Caps followed close by. Down two floors he followed frank to a soundproof room. As the door was about to close when Frank walked in Caps gently pushed on it to make sure it didn't. Placing the box on the table, Frank started pulling out the contents of the box. Knives and saws were coming out one by one. Caps picked up a trophy that was given to the music studio he was in and knocked Frank Senior out cold. Looking around to see what he could tie Frank Senior up with, he noticed that he wasn't standing in a music studio. It was changed into a torcher room.

Vices, knives, picks, razors, leather straps, and all sorts of torcher devices were there. A table that had straps where hands and feet clearly would be was by the door.

Looking in the box Caps found duct tape. After tying up the old man, Caps went back upstairs to his cousins. He was passed his 8 minutes and needed to tell them who he had captured. Back on the main floor and walking up to the bathrooms he then sees Frank Junior. He can't believe his eyes. Junior runs into the bathroom crying. Caps follows.

Walking in he can her Frank talking to himself as he washes his face in the sink.

"Who does that cunt think she is! I got her here. If it weren't for me, she'd be nothing!"

Grabbing a nearby Paper towel Frank dry's his face up and looks in the mirror to see Caps behind him. Quickly he turns around while grabbing his pistol. But Caps is too close. With both hands Caps grabs Frank by the skull and slams his head into the concrete wall, knocking out Junior.

Picking him up, he throws Frank over his shoulder. He walks out of the bathroom as people are walking in. Without hesitation Caps tells them "My friend here had too much to drink." Not that they cared. All of them just walked right past and paid him no mind.

Moments later, Junior wakes up strapped down to a hospital bed.

"Bro! What the fuck is this shit!? Help!?"

"They can't hear you" Caps says leaning on a desk.

Frank junior looks around the room and knows where he is. He wants to move his head but can't budge in his tight restraints. But he knows whose voice it is.

"Bro. . .is that you? How the fuck?"

Caps walks over to where his eyes can see him standing over. A light is right above his face. It's the same one that dentists use. Caps moves it so its more blinding.

"Bro, how the fuck you get here?"

Caps annoyed snaps at him.

"OK! For obvious reasons, I, AM, NOT, YOUR, BRO! Got it? Jesus Christ! You use that word like it's a comma in a sentence. Are you even educated? You sound like a Staten Island stereotype."

Frank Junior answers back equally annoyed. "Go fuck yourself Bro!"

Caps then stabs him in the leg with a screwdriver before responding back.

“Say that, one more time” He then twists the screwdriver. Frank junior screams in pain.

“Somebody! Help!”

Caps knocks on the walls. Then points to the sign that reads “Recording studio”. Stabbing him in the other leg Caps thanks him sarcastically for making this room for him.

“Wait bro. Just wait. I know where she is man. I’m done with her.”

Caps stops twisting the screw drivers and listens. Pulling it out he waits a few seconds for Junior to catch his breath.

“Bro you sure you wanna do this? You sure you want someone back that lied to you from the beginning?”

Getting agitated by Juniors stalling, Caps spins the bed around a few times. Stopping it only to put juniors head in a vice.

“No! Wait Bro! Wait!” He screams as Caps tightens the vice.

Once he was secure and unable to move the bed by squirming back and forth Caps waits and listens.

Frank realizing this was the end started to laugh. Then went back to his trash talking ways.

"She did everything I asked. I even fucked her raw when I was hitting hit from behind. She didn't even know! You gonna die soon bro! Once my father finds me, I'll. . ."

Caps smiles and points to the chair. Holding up a mirror for him he sees his father tied to a chair. His mouth is gagged with a sock and tape. He listened the whole time, trying to make a plea.

"No bro please not him. Come on man! He didn't do anything!"

Caps then walks up to Frank Senior and rips off the tape and pulls out the sock. Grabbing a chair, he sits right between the two Franks and asks two questions.

"Is this true?"

Senior answers after taking a few breaths "I really had nothing to do with what he was doing. I swear it. I knew your father. Please I know my son is a fuck up. He was just trying to do what he thought was right and-"

Caps holds out his finger to get him to stop talking. Then asks his second question.

"Did you know what he was doing?"

Frank Senior with tears in his eyes shook his head yes.

"So, you just fucking let him do whatever the fuck he wants? No guidance at all? Just let him manipulate girls who are having trouble in a relationship?"

Caps gets up and throws his chair at junior. He then turns back to Frank senor and shouts at him.

"Heck what the fuck am I saying? People fucking died because of your shitty parenting!"

Junior tries to reason with him.

"Bro! I am not the one you should be mad at here. It's her. She did this ok?"

Picking up a rubber hammer Caps screams and swings it into Juniors teeth. Breaking the front top row.

"SHUT! THE! FUCK! UP!" He screamed at his hit.

Other than the sound of junior spitting out his teeth the room fell silent. Pulling back his chair Caps sat down and rubbed his fingers on his temples.

A few minutes passed before he asked another question.

"How do I get to where she is without being spotted?"

"You can't" Junior responded.

"Each hallway is guarded by a different gang. All except those Manhattan fags. Bro, you ain't getting to her"

Senior then begs to for his son's life. "Please let my son live. He's a fuck up I know. I'm sorry. He's. . ."

Caps stops him in mid-sentence and points to him and then to Junior asking one final question.

"How long did you know. . . let that go on for?"

"They knew each other before you and Paige met. He used to give her weed and get her high. It's how he gets laid. Please. Let us go."

Blinded by rage Caps pulls out his pistol and points it at Juniors head. He cocks back the hammer. Frank Senior shouts and begs for his son's life. That's when he hears a scream coming from the father. Turning around he sees Senior having a heart attack. A moment later he dies. Checking his pulse. He tells Junior the news.

Junior lays there in silence. Shock begins to set in. He pulls on his restraints, trying to break free. But it's no good. Screaming he yells, demanding to be let free to check on his father.

"You did this! You killed him! Fuck you and your whore!"

Caps starts cutting Frank Senior lose. Using a knife, the cuts off all the duct tape. Then pushes his chair next to his son.

"Your father will be waking up soon."

Junior looks at him with wide eyes, then tries to look at his father. He knows he hasn't been bit.

"He's unconscious?

"No" Caps replied.

Leaning close to his ear he tells him what is going to happen.

"We all come back. Bitten or not. Guess you should have paid more attention in training than on my girlfriend huh?"

Frank doesn't respond. He tries harder to get out. With all his strength he pulls. His wrists and ankles start to bleed from the tension. His eyes try to look down to see how he can get his limbs free.

Then that's when he hears the door close, then lock. A few minutes go by and the lights turn off by themselves. He's scared to make a sound. His father could wake up at any moment.

He hears shuffling and a groaning sound coming from the floor. The sound of tools falling off of something. Suddenly the automatic motion lights come on. His father turns around and sees his son.

Franks screams "NO DADDY NOO!" As his father bites down on his legs. He rips his son apart. Slowly.

Outside no one was there. No sound was heard. Caps was already upstairs, meeting with his cousins.

"Hope you found some way to get to her." Pete says as he grabs his cousin arm and pulls him to the bar.

"I think they're looking for us. Extra guards are near the emergency exits." Pete says points.

Chris runs up to them saying the same thing. Both his cousins look at him smiling. He has lipstick and hickey marks all over his neck.

"Well. . . glad to see you blended in nicely."

“Hey above us. They’re gone. I think it’s time for us to scrub this mission. They suspect something.”

“I’ve got an idea. Chris get those girls to come over here. The ones you were dancing with.”

Running over to them without hesitation. Chris manages to persuade them to come over and grab a drink. Within moments he was able to convince them to go back to their place. Pete was able to take one by the arm and the escorted them out the front doors they came in. The guards looked at them smiling and impressed. They looked at caps with confusion.

“I’m the uhm, designated driver”

“Whatever” the guard responded.

As the three left with their girls the guard from earlier commented on what he saw to the other guard.

“Guess he really does suck dick.”

Once outside the trio walked them to their apartments. Then said their goodbyes. Immediately they start heading back. The rain was starting to slow down.

Looking around at the building the trio try to see one last time if there was any sign of Paige. That's when they heard a scream.

Moments Earlier

VIP

Upstairs Paige wore her favorite dress. It was black with a white skull across the chest. She remembered how Caps loved it when she wore it. How he said repeatedly that he wanted her. She loved the attention she got when she wore this around him. Now she thought to herself as she looked in the mirror, *Let's see if this works on these men.*

Tyrone walked in the room and looked at her up and down whistling as he did so. Taking the compliment, she then did a little spin for the old man.

"My, my, giiirl. You are looking fine. Oh, this is Shansi. She's our date tonight."

"Our?"

She looked at Tyrone, then at Shansi. Slightly confused by this. Paige thought this was just mostly a nice gesture for the work she did or to calm the fiery attitude she showed earlier. But knowing that she was getting free drinks soon, Paige decided to brush it off as if it was just a joke.

Both Paige and Shansi took him by the arms and walked over to the VIP section. The balcony oversaw the whole club. Topless dancers were dancing in cages that were suspended in the air. The lights were ablaze with colors. A fake mist was on the floor of club. Looking down Paige could see in amazement how the dancing made the lights the mist turns into what seemed like a work of art being made right in front of her.

As time went on and a few drinks went down her throat by Shansi, Paige felt buzzed. A strip pole was by them and both her and Shansi danced and joked around about who's sluttier.

Michael came over and whispered into Paige's ear. Tyrone tried to hide that he was clearly upset by what he just heard. He asked the two ladies if they would mind walking him back to his room.

As they left Michael followed close behind. He kept looking at the two ladies with a smirk. Once at his room Tyrone looked at them and opened the door, gesturing to come in.

As they walked in two bodyguards stood outside the door. Shansi started taking her clothes off and saw Paige not taking anything off.

"What's the matter honey? Not in the mood?"

Paige just looked around the room. Tyrone began groping and kissing Shansi. He pauses for a moment and looks to Paige and tells her,

"I no longer have much use for you. Looks like some of your people made it here."

Then he turns to Michael. "She's all yours".

Paige runs into the next room and tries to shut the door. Michael's boot stopped her.

"Steal toe boots hunny. I like your strength though."

His head sticking in between the door and the door frame like a scene from the movie The Shining, he pushes and knocks Paige down.

"Heeeeeres Mikey!" He says with a crazed look on his face.

He grabs Paige by her arms and tries to kiss her. She fights back. Kicking, scratching, even tried using a headbutt, finally she tried using all her strength to pry his grip. Screaming as she did so.

"Ahhhhhhh!"

Meanwhile outside

Caps looked up. It wasn't hard to miss since most lights where off. He saw Paige pushing off someone.

All three of them point their pistols in at the window. They knew they had to act fast since they were exposed and out in the open. All of them trying to get a good angle for a quick shot.

"I'm sorry man there's no way we can get that guy." Chris says while still pointing his pistol at the window.

"Fucking mother fucker. Come on Paige. Get down women" Pete mumbles.

Caps realizes there isn't much time. He knows he must do something, or he might lose her forever. He asks his cousin to hold his ear. Then leans on his shoulder to make a steady shot. He breaths in deep. Remembering what Jacob taught him on the range, he controlled every breath, looked at any shift in the wind he could see to adjust his aim. Then counted softly,

3. . .2. . . 1, fire, fire

Firing only one shot he hears a man scream, pause, scream, pause again. Next few seconds later they see that same man run screaming into the next room.

Paige's point of view

She kept fighting and pushing but she was not getting weaker. Michael pinned her up against the window ledge. Paige looked down as she felt his cold hands moving up her thigh. She closed her eyes and was about to give up when suddenly her face was covered in something warm

Opening her eyes all she could see what blood. Quickly she wiped it off and saw Michael with his noise taken off.

"AAAAAHHHHHHHH!" He screamed in her face.

He runs to the mirror next to them and looks. Then pauses to take in what he looks like.

"AAAAHHHHH!" He screams again.

Michael looks at Paige one last time. at her blue eyes and screams running out of the room, into Tyrone's bedroom as he's fucking Shansi doggy style, and continues to run out the door.

WHAT THE FUCK JUST HAPPENED? Paige screamed internally.

She looked out the window and saw Caps, Pete, And Chris with their pistols aimed at her window. Quickly she runs to her door and locks it. Running back to her window she yells out to them,

"You can't be here. Run! Go now!"

Slamming noise from the bodyguards makes her jump. But she knows if something were to happen to her that there was no real help for her now. She looked out the window one last time and shouted for them to leave.

"Go! I'll be fine!"

She then goes back to the door and opens it. One of the bodyguards must have went to charge the door since he ran right past her as she opened it. Tyrone stood there naked with Shansi.

Shaking his head, he says to her, "We need to talk about your behavior."

Back outside

The trio ran into the park as fast they could. They could see guards running towards their area. That's when they hear the rifle fire. Claire was shooting from the roof. But not at them. Laying on the other side she fired 3 round burst shots at the guards. Not hitting them but scaring them into cover.

"She must be buying us time. Come on let's go!" Pete shouts.

Going back the way they came they run as fast as their legs allowed. Once at the boat the rifle fire stopped. All three looked back and wondered what happed. Then they heard it. A single shot. They knew what it meant.

Uniting the boat, they put the engine on full speed and headed back to Staten Island. All three tried not to think of all of what just happened.

Chapter 16

Quantity has a quality all of its own.

As the sun started to rise, the trio started to yawn. Exhausted from the long night of partying and fighting all they could think about was getting some rest and some hot food in their belly's.

As they came to the ferry terminal Chris noticed a light shining. Seconds later their boat was being riddled with bullet holes. All of them hit the floor of the boat, Chris kept his head down as he turned the boat around.

"I thought we cleared that place" Chris shouted.

"They must have taken it back while we were gone." Caps said back as he a life saver.

Once out of range Chris steered the boat towards the beach. The dead were waiting for them. With bullet holes sinking the ship, there was no choice but to beach the boat on land.

Slowing down as they approached the water they quickly jumped out and ran towards the parking lot, hoping they could find some cars that could be of use. The dead slowly lumbered behind them. A herd was not forming. Noise from them was so loud that all the growling and biting replaced the calm sounds of the ocean.

One by one they went to cars, checking to see if any were open. Lady luck was not with them this day. Pete grabbed a rock and tried smashing a window of a sedan, hitting the driver's side window twice. But only cracks formed. Caps didn't have any better luck. He tried to break into a tesla. He managed to get in but had no idea how to hot wire it. Chris was able to find an old Toyota from the 80s. Breaking through the back window he was able to squeeze his skinny body through. In less than 2 minutes he was able to get it started.

"Assholes! Get in! We're heading home!"

Jumping, Chris steps on the gas. Pete points his middle finger at the herd following them.

They took every side road they could think of to get home. Richmond terrace, to Western ave, then to 6th ave and onto 5th. Each road they carefully looked out for the dead and the living. Low on ammo and lack of sleep meant they couldn't last long in a fight.

"Finally!" Chris screamed as looked at the giant white tanks near home.

As they pulled up to the gate's trucks and cars full of people were pulling out. All had weapons on them.

Caps waved one of them down and asked, "Hey what's going on?"

Mac stuck his head out the window. He wore a ninja turtle bandanna He shouted back at Caps

"Didn't you hear? We're moving in to hit those fuckers back. Sal's going to be out in a minute. Wait here I'll radio him for ya."

As the last car pulls out Commander Sal Caladonato steps out. He's wearing his old army fatigues with all his army badges and patches on it.

"Your late. Come follow us. I'll give you a briefing when we get there, squad leader."

Caps looked around and saw just his cousins. Confused he replies, "I'm not a squad leader."

Commander Caladonato throws him a patch with the letter SL on it.

"You are now. They might have taken back they outposts you took out. But you and your cousins scared the shit out of them. The twins got hold of their radio frequency while you were gone. Been listening to radio chatter all day and night. We might not have the numbers they have but we are sure as hell going to make it seem like we do. I'll brief you when we get there. Just follow us."

It only took close to 20 minutes to get to their out post at near Clove lake. Perimeters were set up all over the streets and parks. The street they were on was Victory. When moving north on victory to clove rd. it dips lower. Then rises again past clove. It makes for a good defense.

As they pull up to the vines church, Commander Caladonato driver runs over to the trio telling them to get some rest. And that the commander will be calling over have the Squad leaders in 6 hours to discuss the plan.

Raiding a nearby house for clean clothes the trio made themselves at home. They grabbed all the blankets and pillows and moved into the living room. Then there was a knock on the door.

Darin had come to check on them and brought food, water, medical supplies and clean army fatigues.

He brought with him the twins, Mac, Pauline and two new people. Jess and Amanda. The new girls were young. Caps asked why he was stuck babysitting.

“Sal called on anyone who was in good shape. Did matter the age.”

Caps looked at the mirror close by. He looked at Pauline. She was talking to the new girls. Showing them how to load a pistol quickly.

“She doing ok” Caps whispered.

Darin pulled him aside.

“She hasn’t said anything to anyone about what happened to her there. Just your cousin Nadine. But she took some plan B pills. I think she will be ok.”

“Some? How many?”

Shrugging his shoulders and tilting his head Darin replies, “Well she had the box.”

“You know I can hear you guys right?” Pauline shouts from the other room.

Amanda and Jess start laughing at the boy’s conversation.

“Do guys really not know how many come in a box?” Amanda says pointing.

Another knock on the door. Chris opens it up to see three other cousins. Phil, Anthony, and Nadine. All brought food as well.

"I guess I should get going. We'll see you in a few hours Caps. . .Squad leader." Darin says as he shakes Caps hand, congratulating him.

Just as Caps was about to shut the door he shouts to Darin, "Who's in my squad?"

"They're right next to you"

Caps looks at his cousins. He knows he has the perfect team.

Back in Brooklyn

Meat shields

Paige and her mother sit on the cold floor of the basement. Chained and handcuffed together in the same place Pauline once was. They ponder on what to say and do next. Paige's mother Lisa screams out making demands.

"I need to use the bathroom."

A bed pan is then thrown down the hall, landing near her feet. She looks at her daughter then starts to cry.

"Where is that boy Frank. Can't he help us?"

Paige just sits there. Not wanting to answer. She doesn't want to talk about anything. Looking down she sees glass. Picking it up she contemplates killing herself. She looks at her mother. Seeing her crying made her throw the glass away. Leaning over she takes her hand.

"We're going to be ok."

Lisa looks back at her daughter and tries to smile. The door down the hall opens and she looks back to see who's walking down to get them. Two guards unchained them and brought them outside. The air was cold. Neither had jackets or warm clothes to wear. Paige was still in the same dress from the club. Her mother was just in jeans, and a plan blue t-shirt. Both shivered in the cold.

The streets were filled with cars and trucks. Gangs were checking their weapons and counting ammunition. Paige knew what this meant.

"You planning an invasion?" She asked the guards with cold mist coming from her mouth.

Tyrone walks in from behind them. Wearing a fur coat and twirling his cane he replies, "Yes, yes we are. I told you. I own the five boroughs."

A bell started to ring, then every truck, car, and motorcycle started their engines.

“You ladies are staying with me.”

“Why do you want us? Don’t do anything to her. It’s me that hurt your rapist buddy there.”

Michael looks over with bandages where his nose used to be, gives her the finger while driving off.

Tyrone laughs. With his cane he points at them. As he moves closer his face changes to that of anger. As he breaths the cold air creates a mist that comes from his nostrils. Making his anger even more visible.

“Someone you know killed Frank and his father last night. I’m assuming you know who.”

Lisa’s jaw dropped. She squeezed Paige’s hand to comfort her. But Paige felt nothing for him. She despised him for what he did to her. How he used and humiliated her.

“Maybe you were in on this from the beginning, maybe you just had a change of heart. Either way your friends made it through my defenses and made an attempt on my life. So, I need a meat shield. Anything happens to me. . .she dies, and you watch. Then you die. Got it?"

Paige doesn't show any expression. No sorrow or anger. Just a blank look. The guards then pull Paige and Lisa to the truck. Tyrone jumps in his limo and asks for an update on his men crossing the bridge. His driver tells him that the area has been secure. However heavy fighting has been going on Hyln Blvd.

"Where is there the least and most amount of fighting?" He asked while taking a sip of Champaign.

"So far the most I would have to be near the ballpark, but Some of the bloods are taking it as we speak. We lost over 100 men so far Should I ask them to do anything sir?"

Looking at a map with one hand and drinking in the other he contemplates his next move.

"So the least is in the center by Tompkinsville train. Looks like they tried to divide us. How many men we have left so far?

"Between the queens, Bronx, the Manhattan Knights, and our own? About two thousand. But sir we're losing more than we're taking out."

Putting down his drink he marks the locations he just heard. Pondering for a moment he then told his driver.

“The red head did say she had better people than us. Cops and military. . . Well as the Russians say. Quantity has a quality all its own.”

Sir?” The driver asked concerned.

“Nothing never mind what I just said. Order the men to take the Tompkinsville park.”

“Sir why not just take the highway to their HQ? Maybe we can end this quickly.”

“No, no, no. If they had time to set up traps there. Plenty of hiding places on that route where we will be caught in the open. No, if we’re going to fight we might as well do it in a place where our numbers can take an area and hold it without being taken out from a far. Besides I want to see what happens when we unleash the trucks of the dead on them.

“You sure that’s still a good idea? I mean. . .”

“YES, IM SURE!” He loudly responds.

“Those mother fuckers killed and then turned our boys into weapons. That truck they left behind on the bridge. This was their idea to use the dead as a weapon.”

Turing around the driver knew he was overstepping his boundaries.

"Yes sir, understood"

Looking around Tyrone picked up his hand radio and ordered for everyone to cross the bridge and move to Tompkinsville with their trucks full of their new weapon.

After resting

Heading to their temporary HQ, Caps met up with Darin along the way. Walking into the building they sat down Indian style on the floor. Commander Caladonato went over what was currently being done and what their mission will be. Caps, Darin, and the new squad called Amazonians. They were all female group. Their mission was to support the other two squads in taking back the Islamic center. Its tower would help spot the enemy. Other squads were grouped together as well to take other objectives. All

An hour after the briefing. Caps, Darin, and Amazonian Squads moved out. They packed all ammunition that was left for the taking before leaving. M4s and M16s were the only rifles they carried. So ammunition was made easier to distribute since both used the same 5.56 rounds. There were only two grenades for use. Pete had the best throwing arm so one was given to him. Darin held the other. A few sticks of custom-built explosives as well were given out. 3 in each squad. The fuse would only give them about ten seconds before it exploded.

Near their destination they stopped short of Cebra ave Moving through houses and backyards to a wooded area near Castleton ave. From there Caps squad moved into the green and hid. While on the corner of Oxford place and Cerbra, Darin positioned his men in and on the side of the old Morelos deli. The Amazonians stayed on Victory Blvd. and Cebra. They were to start firing to get the attention of the Brooklyn knights there.

At 6pm Amazonians opened fire on the nearby camp in the grocery store next to the large parking lot that reached into the Islamic center. Darin's squad stuck to the plan and ran forward. Building proving much needed cover.

Caps squad moved out of the greenery and into the open street. They tried to cross quickly but in one of the windows he and his squad were spotted. A heavy machinegun opened fire. Anthony became riddled with bullets. Phil was grazed by a few. Both Nadine and Pete went back into cover. Chris and Caps were the only ones to make it to the other side.

Taking cover behind a dumpster Chris yelled over the sound of gun fire.

“Where is everyone?”

“What?” Caps answers back.

“Where is everyone?” Chris tries to ask again but louder.

“No idea”

Meanwhile Darin’s squad was paralyzed with fear over hearing two men get shot. Gun fire began to punch holes in the building they occupied. All put their heads down. Darrin broke open the door and guided everyone outside. A small backyard with a incline was between them and a few open windows. One of which had a Machinegun nest in it. Others where just support with rifles.

Unable to move Darin ran to the front and kept shouting.

“Move come on. Let’s go!”

Then running into the incline on the backyard hill, grabbing some of his men by the arm he pulled them up.

“Come on! Let’s go!” He shouted.

Two men and a woman run forward and to the left. The women ran forward and was shot multiple times in the head within seconds.

The men who moved to the left supported Caps and his cousin as they moved in closer.

"Supporting fire!" They both kept shouting as Caps moved in. Chris takes out his grenade and throws it onto the window ledge. It bounces and hits one of the Brooklyn knights on his shoulder. It explodes, throwing shards of hot metal and broken glass outwards.

From the second floor More gun fire erupted. Then that's when the Amazonians started firing on the second floor.

Darin's troops moved up using the covering fire that the Amazonians provided. Caps and Chris moved around to their side of the building. Nadine and Pete Kept the shooters busy as Caps and Chris used their home-made explosives. Each waited 6 seconds before they threw one into a window.

Now getting cocky, 3 of Darin's men jumped into the window to clear out the building. Kicking in a door they activated a trip wire. A chain of explosives erupted the building. Part of the wall was knocked down. Two of the men lay dead. One started to slowly walk out of the building. It was one of the new guys Darin was given. The young man called out.

"Sir? Darin, is that you?"

His eye was swollen up. Cuts and scrapes were all over his face and chest. Giant gashes were on his legs. Stepping out of the building covered in not just his blood, he stumbles and then collapses to the floor.

Mac sees him and comes to his side. Holding him close he tells him “Relax buddy. You’re gonna be alright. Ok were gonna get you fixed up ok.”

Nadine and Pete make it across the street. Phil stays behind offer supporting fire on the windows. As they jump in through the bottom windows the Brooklyn knights start running. Retreating through the open parking lot, many of them ran for their cars. That’s when the Amazonians started mowing them down from the grocery store. They had cleared it out instead of just keeping them busy. Nearly 60 Brooklyn knights were killed. 7 Staten islanders were killed and two wounded.

After radioing in their casualties and telling HQ that they got their objective, trucks began to show up. All three squads opened fire. But no gun fire was sent back in return. Suddenly the gates in the back of the trucks opened up. A horde of infected came running out towards them. 5 of Amazonians squad was taken down. Everyone else made it inside the mosque and locked the door.

"How long you think till they find out they can go through the side?" Pauline shouted with her back on the door.

As many shot the infected from the window's they noticed in the distance more trucks. Just waiting to be unloaded. That's when Darin got the order to fall back on hero park.

Falling back was not going to be easy. More vehicles started showing up in the distance. They were waiting for the infected to be killed so they could move in. It was now starting to get dark. The last of the horde fell under Mac rifle fire.

Moving through the back windows and into the greenery they moved up hill. Each squad covering the other in turns.

Coming up to Stanly street they met with another squad. Legion squad. Mostly made up of retired swat cops, they wore their own body armor. They trained to clear out buildings. Usually they were given the hard task of clearing buildings off of Stanley street, where dead were known for still being in large groups. Today they were tasked to clear out the living.

With armor shields and a few flash grenades they kept the Brooklyn knights at bay. A minute into the fighting the knights fell back to the Islamic center.

"Who's in charge here? I don't see Keenan" Darin asked.

Keenon walked forward with a limp. He was a tall man with a thick bushy beard. His eyes green as jade. A blood-stained bandage covered his leg. Everyone knew what it was.

"In that building behind us, I got bit. These fuckers really did manage to use the dead as weapons."

Both Darin and Pauline looked at him and wanted to help. Amanda from the Amazonian squad took out a blow torch to burn the wound. But the retired cop refused.

"I was already going my dear. Cancer had been draining me all year."

Amanda looked at her squad leader but there was no response. No one could order him to take the burn. Due to his skinny frame he might just collapse and die anyways. But he was still in charge of this sector. So, no one questioned his logic.

"Where's your third squad leader. Caps isn't it?"

Looking around no one saw any site of him. Some called out his name. No response.

"You think he got lost? Or went to Hero park?" Pauline asked.

Keenon took a step forward and informed them of how that wasn't possible.

Hero park has been over run. They moved in about an hour ago. Commander Caladonato has been drawing the enemy onto that area for the past hour.

More gun fire suddenly whizzed past their heads. Brooklyn knights were making another attempt to take Stanly st. Seconds after everyone dropped to the ground and engaged the enemy, explosions started in front of them. Brooklyn knights had an abundance of grenades.

Pauline and one of the girls from Amazonian squad went over to a nearby tree. Pauline lifted her up so she could shoot from the treetops. Giving her more of an elevated position. Returning fire from her elevated position the Amazonian fired ten shots, killing eight, wounding two. Pauline looked on in awe at her aim. Then she saw her body drop from the tree. A gaping hole was in the center of her head.

I didn't even learn her name. Pauline thought to herself.

Suddenly the shooting stopped. The Brooklyn knights fell back once again. Darin wanted to pursue them but Keenon talked him out of it.

"Our orders are to fall back."

As they retreated fires started erupting. Commander Caladonato ordered a scorched earth policy when falling back. The legion started taking cans of gas and throwing it on building nearby. With a match Keenon ignited a whole block. Fashion shops, delis, and churches were set ablaze. Looking in the distance was something they weren't expecting. The Brooklyn knights were also setting fires. Darin got on the radio and asked his commander to stop the order.

"They aren't here just for conquest! They are here to exterminate us!" Darin yelled into the radio as they headed to Hero park. He knew his friend, his commander had something planned. Otherwise he wouldn't have ordered what is technically a fighting retreat.

Moments earlier

As gun fire broke out around them, Phil fell behind. His leg was badly injured in earlier fighting. Near him was the man Mac helped earlier. But he wasn't moving. Caps stayed and tried his best to stay low to the ground while pulling his cousin to safety. But the Brooklyn knights surrounded him. Phil shot three of them before his weapon jammed. Taking out his knife he swung back and forth trying to keep the attackers away. But it was no use. Caps was knocked out by the back of a rifle. A few Brooklyn knights held Phil down, then picking up Phil's knife, a Brooklyn knight named Duke grabs Phil by the hair, pulls his head back and slices his throat open.

Seeing the fight not going their way they fall back. Duke seeing a navy see bag, runs towards it like a kid who just saw free candy being given out. He tries to pick it up quickly but the weight of his makes it difficult. With the help of a fellow comrade they manage to bring it back to the mosque. Unzipping it they find ammunition, rations, and tons of medical supplies. Realizing that there must be more he convinces his new leader Michael to try again. That they knocked out someone along the way. They could use him for information.

Michael wanting blood for what had happened to him the night before didn't hesitate to order another attack.

"As we move in, I want you and your buddy here to grab whoever it is you knocked out and bring them to hero park. Question him there while we move up into clove lake."

Another attack was ordered. Duke grabs Caps unconscious body and with the other Brooklyn knight they quickly tie him up, putting him in the navy sea bag. Immediately they drag him back towards the mosque.

"Alrighty! Head towards hero park. Tyrone will be here shortly. We cleared out that area. I got orders to head to clove lake."

The tow throw Caps into the car and drive to Hero Park. The night sky was lite up by fires in the distance.

Opening the car door, they start dragging the sea bag into the park. The Manhattan skyline can be seen in the distance. Along with the northern end of Staten Island that was now on fire. It brightened the night sky. Just then a kick from the bag. They realize that Caps is awake.

"Come on Duke. I think this a good enough spot as any."

"Yeah ok. Dump him"

Grabbing the bottom of the bag and dumping the man headfirst onto the dirt, the Brooklyn Knights laughed at his pain.

Though he was now awake he could barely hear what the knights were saying to him. His ears were ringing from the explosions in the earlier battle. When one of the knights pointed to what was going on in the distance Caps looked, he saw the fires. He stares at the blazing houses. He listens to the gun fire, the car tires screeching as the rubber and pavement grind against each other in the distance. The screams of people in pain. Even from this distance he could make out some words.

One of the Brooklyn Knight's loses his patience. Duke takes out the knife he obtained earlier and starts pointing it at the fires in the distance. Then grabs Caps by the shirt collar and yells into his ear.

His hearing was starting to come back, but the yelling didn't help. He made out some words. Duke quickly cut Caps cheek. He jerks his head in the opposite direction to avoid the blade as best he could. The Brooklyn Knight laughed as he showed off the knife. Then the other one says, "You got nothing to say huh?

Caps looks around him and listens. He look's left, then right, then smiles widely. He knows where he is. And what they just walked into.

“The fuck you smiling at cock sucker!” One of them shouts.

Suddenly lights turn on all around them. The Brooklyn Knights look around in every direction and pull out their pistols. They shout, “Mother fuckers! Put down your weapons mother fuckers!”

They see a dozen shadowy figures. All with bows and rifles pointed at them. They don’t say anything.

“You shit heads want us? Huh?!” The two Brooklyn Knight’s shouted as some of the shadowy figures walked towards them.

Too busy pointing their guns at everything that walked towards them, they don’t realize that Caps untied himself. He then stands up behind them and puts on his glasses. They both turn around in a frantic panic and point their guns at him. Each of their reflections shines in a lens of his glasses. They see the fear they are showing.

Caps keeps smiling and says calmly. “I got something to say. You boys make a lot of noise. You forget where you are? Welcome to the quiet borough.”

Mac comes from behind them, knocking their heads together. They fall the floor unconscious. Caps picks up his cousins’ knife and stabs one of the Brooklyn knights in the head. As he's about to kill the other one Sal shouts for him to stop.

"Hold it! We need this one alive. You catch his name?"

"Duke, I think"

Then Sal signals for everyone to go back to their positions. Caps follows close behind his commander.

"What's the plan now?" Caps asked.

"In about a minute the leader is coming here. We captured a few of their men. We blocked their radio chatter with some help from the twins. They think the way is clear. Whoever this Tyrone guy is, he's been sending in these trucks of infected in first? We got something to counter that on the hills of Victory Blvd. Stay close to me. Got it?"

"Yes sir" Caps replied.

Right on cue the trucks arrived. Makeshift chairs were put on top of the vehicles. Gunners with machine guns sat on top of the trucks.

Commander Sal Caladonato gave a hand signal to the man in the outpost. They then followed the order he gave and fired blue and green flairs shot up into the night sky.

Cars without drivers were now going downhill on Victory Blvd. As the trucks reached Hero Park they were hit by a dozen cars, which then blew up instantly. The explosions weren't enough to destroy the trucks, but that wasn't the goal. The truck's cab where the engine and driver were, was now destroyed in the two leading trucks. They began to roll back down the steep road that was Victory, knocking into other trucks as they did so.

All the cars and pickup trucks that had Brooklyn knights in them were hit like dominos. Commander Sal Caladonato watched through binoculars at the carnage with a smile on his face. He then hands the binoculars over to Caps. As he looks through them, he watches how some of the trucks back doors opened. Releasing freshly infected people. They tore into the knights. The he saw a limo that was pinned down. A woman broke through the window, she then helped another out. It was Paige. She was able to get away but was being chased by a group of women. The Amazonians must have made their way there. Caps quickly jumped to his feet and started running down Victory to get to her before they did.

Almost over.

Before and during the ambush

Moving through his newly conquered land, Tyrone came to the conclusion that he could lose them again. Now in an almost drunken state, he ordered his men to start burning the town houses and any nearby buildings.

As time passed, he became bored waiting for the smoke to clear. Getting on the radio he asked, “Bring me the women and her mother.”

Stopping traffic guards brought Paige over. The limo doors were opened and bother Paige and her mother were forced in. Paige sat on the left of Tyrone, her mother on the right. The guards sat on in the front end of the limo.

“You know, I never had a threesome with a mother and daughter before.”

Both looked away from him in disgust. His breath reeked of alcohol.

Loud explosions were then heard. Tyrone grabbed his radio and shouted for answers. But there were no answers. Again, and again he tried but nothing. Ordering his guards to get out and check he grabbed Paige’s leg.

"You are staying right here with me sugar."

As the first guard step's out a truck hits him. Taking both him and the limo door. Another truck then rolls right onto the limo. Killing the other guard instantly. The sudden impact causes Tyrone to hit his head against Lisa's.

Wasting no time Paige jumps out through the window. Pulling her mother out with her.

Quickly they run down Victory and towards anywhere that isn't on fire or have people chasing them. Stopping only for a second when she sees Pauline with some others. At first, she smiles and thinks to herself, *Oh thank God*. Her hopes turn into a nightmare when Pauline raises her rifle and takes a shot in her direction.

Not sure who to trust

Paige ducks for cover. She pulls her mother by then hand, trying to get her to run faster. But it's no use. She falls and twists her ankle. Lisa tells her daughter to run.

Amazonian squad quickly catches up. Some stay behind and secure Lisa. Pauline, Amanda, and Jess chase Paige down Victory. She runs into a clothing shop nearby. Knocking down manikins, racks of cloths and boxes to buy herself some time. Realizing she can't outrun them, she crouches down, trying to hide. The female trio raises their rifles and turns on their lights.

"Come out traitor!" Pauline shouts.

Paige looking at a downed Manikin takes off its shoes and puts them on. Her feet were bleeding from the barefoot running she did seconds ago.

Taking a head of a manikin, Paige throws it across the room, knowing over a rack of clothes. The female trio opens fire in that direction. Knowing her chance to escape is now she runs out the back door and into alleyways. She continues close to victory.

Her mind races. She has no one now. No friends, no family, nothing. I want it all to end! Thoughts of suicide set in. Then out of the smoke she sees the apartment buildings near the water.

I just need to hide out and think of what to do next. She thought to herself.

Thirty minutes of none stop running and walking she finally made it. She knew this place was clear since it was Caps who did it months ago.

Rifle fire then went passed her head. Ducking Paige looked back to see Pauline running towards her with two others. Caps was in the distance running towards her as well. She quickly ran inside and up the stairs.

“Oh GOD! This is it!” She screamed while running.

The trio followed close behind. Randomly shooting up the stairs hoping to get a lucky shot.

Paige went as far up as she could. Now on the roof she tried to lock the door behind her, but here was no lock. Only a broken chain. She backed up to the ledge. Her heart raced and all thought left her mind as she watched the door open. Pauline and the other stepped through, rifles aimed.

As the trio approaches Paige kept stepping backwards. Her mind so occupied at what they will do to her she loses her footing and trips on broken ceiling tile, falling off the side.

Pauline and Amanda are pushed aside. Caps jumps over, with one hand on the ledge and the other holding onto Paige's ankle he shouts, "Pull!"

Pauline looks over the ledge and holds onto caps, as does the others.

"What are you doing? Let her-"

Caps not wanting to hear it shouts back, "I SAID PULL! NOW!"

Pulling so hard that they fall over once Paige is back on the roof. Caps exhausted, sits down, leaning his back on the wall. Sweat covering his head felt cold from the weather outside. He looked at his breath turn into mist. He looked at Paige, she was shivering. PTSD and the cold made her curl up in the fetal position. Caps took off his Jacket and put it in her.

"Come on. Let's get you inside"

"Pauline looked at him confused. She can't believe what she was seeing. As he walked her inside, Pauline stood up and grabbed him by the arm.

"You really are glutton for punishment, aren't you?"

Caps didn't respond. Just pulled his arm back and walked Paige inside.

War is over. Go home

The battle came to a close. On the radio, there was chatter that the leader of the Brooklyn knights was captured, but had to be shot since he was bitten multiple times.

Caps met back up with his cousins and headed back home. He didn't go back to the prison. He went to his actual home. The home he grew up in. His cousins came with him. Paige slept the entire ride.

When they turned off Bloomindale Sal was there, waiting. Paige woke up and saw what was going on.

"Wait here." Caps said to Paige. Nadine stayed in the car with her.

Walking up to his commander he stood at ease. He waited for Sal to speak first. And he did.

"You know we have to take her in, don't you?"

Caps stood there silently. His cousins with their hands on their Pistols. Sa's men didn't raise their rifles, but they were ready as well. Not answering made the situation tense.

Sal walks into arm's length. He leans over and says one thing.

“Hope she’s worth it private” He says with a smile of approval.

Not caring about his demotion caps still stood their silently. His cousins were ready to fight, even knowing they wouldn’t win.

Taking a step back Sal smiles again and tells Caps, “Come back when you’re ready.”

With that he turns around and walks back to his Humvee. He drives off with his men.

Turning around Caps takes a deep breath in to calm his nerves.

Moments later after unpacking and getting ready for bed Paige notices him taking pillows into the next room.

“Where you going?” She asks.

Stopping at the door he replies, “I figure you wanted to be left alone”

“Wait!” She shouts when he gets closer to the door.

She runs up to him. Hugging him tightly. She puts her head against his chest and listens to his heartbeat.

“I’m sorry. I’m sorry for everything.”

“I know. I am too.” Caps replied.

They stand there for a moment, just hugging. Caps then gives her some good news.

“Your mom is alright. She’s being questioned but Sal told me on the radio that nothing will happen to her. I’ll pick her up tomorrow.”

Paige looks up with her big blue eyes. She pulls him by the shirt collar and kisses him. Caps drops his pillow. They sleep in the same bedroom.

Over the next few weeks

After the Brooklyn knights surrendered new local government formed in Brooklyn. Each borough now was free to trade and govern as they wished. Negotiations now took place over the next few weeks. Prisoners were exchanged and gang members were either imprisoned or sentenced to death. Most squads stood together.

Caps tried his best to start a new life as a trader. But the constant need for raiding and seeing scouts made it almost impossible to settle down.

Though the short war was over, life didn't change too much. Everyone was used to loss. Death didn't shock most of them.

A week before thanksgiving Caps reported back to the Prison. The HQ was cleaner than he remembered. New maps were on the walls and new faces were around in the HQ.

An old voice was heard on the radio that Greg and rob operated.

"Staten Island! Come in. This is Sergeant Stiff over! Is anyone there?"

Rob grabbed the headset right off his brother's head. The wire smacking his brother across the face as he did so.

"Holy shit! Stiffffay! That you!?"

"It's Stiff, and yes it's me. I need Commander Caladonato on now."

Rob punches his brother in the shoulder in excitement. "Oh man sure thing buddy. You finally coming back? Oh, by the way missed one hell of a party."

"Yes. I'm bringing some new friends too."

Some weeks after returning to work

Soon after reporting back to work Caps found himself scouting and raiding places near the ferry terminal. Sitting down near the ledge he waited for his old friend Pauline. Looking out into the city he wondered what the group out there is like. He knew they weren't much for fighting since the war. But he remembered what it was like going out into Manhattan before the world ended. When the war was going on the old smell of what the city used to be like was somewhat in the air. Sounds too. Tires screeching, gasoline fumes. These small things brought him back to a time that seemed like ages ago. Now it was gone.

"Hey cuz, she's here. I'll leave you two alone. Come Petey boy."

"Please for fuck sake, stop calling me that"

"You got it side kick" Chris says patting his shoulder.

"I fucking hate you" Pete says rolling his eyes.

Laughing at what she heard Pauline sits next to Caps. He wasn't laughing. Just brooding.

"You doing alright Cappy?"

Smoking a cigar, he hands her a letter that was slightly burned.

As Pauline unfolded it, she asked him about the burn marks.

"Guessing you were burning this but had second thoughts, huh?"

He nodded yes as he took another puff.

Once opened Pauline read in silence. The letter read.

Johnny

I'm sorry. I have to leave. I just can't stay here anymore. I know life was hard as a trader and you were bored. But going back to that job made memories of my mistakes come back. I cheated on you because I thought you didn't appreciate me. You were always busy. When you were in school before all this I understood, but I still felt like you didn't care. That all you cared about was your own self. I know now that I was wrong. I know it doesn't mean much for you to know this since I wont say it to your face but I regret it what I did Even after all this time it still hurts.

Also, your friends keep looking at me like I can't be trusted. I don't blame them. What I did was wrong, and I should have talked to you. But now I feel like it's too late. You might not care what others think, but I do.

I decided to take my chances and go out to Jersey, maybe even further out. If Sergeant Stiff and Jack can do it with little supply's, they had then so can I. Don't worry. I'm not going alone. I'm taking my mother and some friends who used to work in the 123 precinct.

I did love you. I know how hard you tried to make things better and that you wanted to give me more attention when you were less busy. I should have paid more attention to that. How you tried to get me to communicate more instead of retreating from tough conversations. But I need to work on myself for a while. Take care of yourself. Maybe I'll come back someday.

After reading the note she hands it back to Caps. She watches as he burns it with his cigar. Then she looks back and sees his truck. Its filled with food and supplies. She tries to guess his next move.

"Either you just went on a raid or you're going after her. Which is it Johnny boy?"

He doesn't answer her question. Instead he smiles and looks at the train tracks nearby. Then gets up telling her,

"I got you a gift. Come with me. I'll explain on the way.

Score

Walking up to the door Caps grabs the handle, he turns it open but stops to ask Pauline one last time if she's ready.

"OK, you ready? Remember what I told you to do. OK? You got this?"

Pauline smiles with a wink before responding, "Yeah I got this."

Stepping into the dark room a man tied up to a bed shouts loudly, "Whose there?" Pauline turns on the light and removes his blindfold. His face is a wreck. His noise is missing. She almost didn't recognize him. It was her rapist Michael.

"Welllllll. . . Look who it is. You want some more honey?" Michael says with a sinister yellow smile.

Even though the thought of this man disgusts her she played along in the plan.

"Yeah baby I'm all yours" She says slowly putting her leg over him.

She starts plating with his beard and hair. She nibbles on his ear lobe and whispers to him.

“You miss my tight ass?”

Michael tries to grab her ass, but his restraints stop him. So, he moves his hips in a humping motion.

“Easy baby. Let me ride you” She says with a wink.

Slowly she pulls the covers over them and kisses him. First on the neck, then shoulders, his chest, and keeps going down till she’s under the covers. Michael is now rock hard.

“Fuck yeah. I knew you wanted this dick!”

Then just as it seemed Pauline was about to go down on her she vanishes. The sound of a door creaking open can be heard. The room was suddenly dark again.

Aggravated he screams, “Hey! What the fuck!” Get back here and suck me off!”

Suddenly under the sheet a head shape starts to form. It moves closer to his crotch.

“Yeah baby. That’s it! Come to poppa!”

He feels cold flesh touch his foreskin.

"That's new. Ow. Easy there honey. Wait, Ow! Ow! Ahhhhh! Ahhhhhh!"

Pauline then stands up from behind the bed, turning on the light and ripping off the sheets to show who's under.

Seeing Pauline at the door made him look down to see who was at his crotch. It was Sabrina. Caps then let go of the restraints that held her away from himself but in the direction he wanted. She then chomped down with all her might. Michael screamed in pain, begging to make it stop. Sabrina looked up at her killer. Her dead eyes locking with Michaels. Pauline and Caps run out the door. Closing it behind them, they could hear Michael screaming, begging for mercy.

Leaning his back against the wall, Caps stood from across from Pauline. Both were out of breath from that short burst of adrenaline but smiled.

"Feel better now?" He asked.

"Oh yeah." She says with a nervous laugh.

Caps watched her crouch down to the floor. Just looking at her he could tell that the rush of adrenalin from killing her rapist felt good. Wanting to make sure she didn't think about it too much and fall back into depression, he tried to change the subject.

"Let's get lunch. I heard they got recess for snack in the mess hall."

Looking up at him she responds, "You always do try to make a bad situation into a good one. Eh Johnny boy?"

To be continued. . .

Comics

Darin Joseph

Army Veteran, Comedian.
https://www.youtube.com/watch?v=CTwTABiiwmU

Greg and Rob

Host of the Greg and Rob podcast that can be found on YouTube, Facebook and Spreaker.
https://www.youtube.com/watch?v=B6CtV1JE4NE

Joseph W Mac

Comedian, Comic book artist, and background actor.

https://www.youtube.com/watch?v=D-jah4b_CzA

John Kuschner

https://www.youtube.com/watch?v=tVXSibt1hbI

James Mac

Army Veteran, Comedian

www.hsntcomedy.com

Pauline Murphy

Comedian

https://www.youtube.com/watch?v=yERYJiOPJH4

Sal Coladonato

Army veteran, Comedian, Host of the “Slant podcast” which can be found on YouTube and Facebook.

Made in the USA
Middletown, DE
03 May 2020

92498362R00139